DYING FOR DINNER ROLLS

A GEORGIA COAST COZY MYSTERY (BOOK 1)

LOIS LAVRISA

Enjoy ☺
Lois Lavrisa

SUNLAKE PRESS

In memory of my "City Grandma" Anna Donna Siminuk Piwowar—a character in the tenth degree. When she dressed up, she would wear dyed fabric pumps to coordinate with her chiffon dresses—one in every color and always accessorized with rhinestone jewelry. For twenty years, she waitressed at the State Street Chicago Marshall Field's restaurant, making friends with all who stopped by. Anna and her two sisters, Helen Olsen and Mary Schmaus, would lip sync and dance to the Andrews Sisters' records. They were fabulous entertainment at parties. Anna believed that all men were frogs (no matter how much you kiss them, no prince would ever materialize), and a woman only had to pick the nicest frog. She never got a chance to meet my husband, Tom, but I know she would agree that I followed her advice.

JOIN THE NEWSLETTER

If you'd like to receive the latest news and information about my upcoming books, please sign up for my free author newsletter at:

loislavrisa.com/newsletter

CHAPTER 1

"When are you due, sweetie?" a petite gray-haired lady asked me as I bagged her groceries.

"Um, I'm not…" I looked down at my shirted belly.

Andrew, my husband, handed the customer her credit card slip and chuckled. "If she's pregnant, she's going to have some explaining to do."

The lady signed the slip and passed it back to Andrew. "Is that so?"

"Cat's my wife." Andrew gave the grocery bag to her. "After two sets of twins, I visited the urologist."

I jabbed Andrew in the side. Sometimes he had no filter.

"Cat?" the lady asked.

"Catherine Alice Thomson," I replied. "Everyone calls me Cat."

The lady took her bag and turned to me. "Sorry I implied you're—"

"Fat?" I asked.

"Oh, no, dear. You couldn't be more than a hundred pounds." The lady waved her hand. "And I just love this health food store. It's so lovely."

"Thank you," I called after her as she exited the store. I smoothed down the poufs in my shirt. "That's it. I have to stop wearing this billowy top even though it's all the rage. This style

1

only looks good on six-foot-tall, rail-thin models, not normal-sized people like me."

Andrew kissed the top of my head. "You're glowing. That's what I'm sure she meant. And tasty, too."

"Huh?" I asked.

He grabbed a lettuce leaf stuck to my bright yellow apron with our store's name on it: Sunshine Market. The name came from the song "You Are My Sunshine," which was my parents' wedding song.

Andrew asked, "Cat, can you straighten that display while I put new register tape in?"

"No problem." I tucked my shoulder-length black hair behind my ears and got to work.

A few moments later, a police officer walked past our store and nodded to Andrew and me.

I turned to Andrew. "You know, the police still haven't reopened the case about that night. And they just hired a few new officers. Maybe they could look into it. You know. New eyes on the case?"

Andrew knew what "that night" meant—the night my dad was killed. Actually, all of my friends knew what I meant when I said "that night." Two months ago, while my dad worked late and alone at the store, he'd been shot.

After my father's death, Andrew, knowing how much work there would be now that my dad had died, had decided to quit his job as an architect to help my mom and me run the family business. My mom still did the bookkeeping and accounting for our Savannah, Georgia organic health food store.

I'd worked at the store practically my entire life. Now, though, I found it difficult to spend a lot of time there. Memories of my dad were tucked away on every wooden shelf lining the walls and on every inch of the reclaimed heart pine floor. Sometimes I thought I smelled his Old Spice cologne lingering in the air.

As an only child, I'd been hit hard by my dad's death. My mom still grieved, saying she would never love another human being as much as she'd loved my father. Although she mourned, she rolled up her sleeves and got back to work. She said she had to honor her husband's store by keeping it successful.

Work distracted my mom from the loss of her husband. Whereas my grief manifested in the form of my determination to catch his killer.

Andrew rang up a customer's groceries, the beep sounding as each item crossed the scanner.

A few moments later, the customer left.

Andrew turned toward me. "Honey, I know how much this hurts you, but I keep telling you the police did all they could. What happened to your dad was a horrible tragedy."

"You know I can't let go until I have answers."

"Do what you need to do. I'll support you, no matter what. But I'm afraid you'll just keep opening old wounds."

"It happened two months ago, not two years. The wounds are not that old. Plus, the killer could still be lurking around."

"You're safe now," Andrew said. "We'll catch anyone doing anything with the new surveillance cameras and security system."

"I just wish we'd had all of that earlier. Maybe that night wouldn't have happened. He'd still be alive."

Andrew gave me a hug. "I wish he were still here, too."

"I keep thinking that maybe if I'd stayed late and worked with him, rather than him closing the store by himself, it wouldn't have happened." I took a deep breath, replaying the what-ifs in my head as I had a million times already. Thinking that somehow, someway, I could undo the events of that night, and he'd still be alive.

Andrew rang up another customer. Then he offered the customer a pen to sign the credit card slip, but the customer held up a purple pen that he already had.

A purple-inked crossword puzzle had been found under my dad's body. And there'd been no purple pen in sight in the store. Additionally, my dad never did the crossword. Several blocks had been filled in, spelling "sweet revenge," which hadn't seemed like a relevant clue.

But that puzzle pointed to my dad's murderer. I just knew it.

3

Although the police had concluded, after a brief investigation, that my father's death was simply a burglary gone bad, I had not. I hung on to the crossword puzzle as the sole lead to the killer.

After the customer left, I elbowed Andrew. "Purple pen."

Andrew shook his head and sighed. "See? You're going to drive yourself—and *me,* for that matter—crazy. Since that night, you've hovered over every person you see doing a crossword puzzle. You think that everyone with a purple pen is a suspect. You need to let it go."

But I couldn't let it go. My sense of justice prevailed over reason. Not only because the killer had taken away my dad, but also because he might intend to harm other people in my life. I felt that I had to keep vigil to protect my loved ones.

I glanced at the framed picture near the register. It showed my mom and dad, his arm over her shoulder, both of them smiling at the photographer. Their striking difference—my tall father's light complexion and blond hair and my short mom's dark, Asian coloring—never bothered them.

My mom, Yunni, walked over to me and gave me a hug. "You restock produce now. We got new delivery." Yunni tapped her thumb with mine.

She still spoke in half-broken English, as she was born in Korea. My American dad had met her forty-five years ago while he was in the service. She stood about four feet, ten inches tall in heels and had thick, black hair cut short in layers, big brown eyes, and a smile that took up half her face. My thick hair was like hers, but I looked more like my father, who was born to Welsh and Irish parents.

Tapping our thumbs together was our private signal connecting us to my dad. My dad had two wedding bands that he'd alternated wearing, depending on his mood. When he was in his Sunday-best mood, his choice was the platinum band with the diamonds, which my mom now had on her thumb, and I wore the plain gold band that he'd favored when he felt casual. Since my dad had a much thicker ring finger than my mom and me, his wedding bands would only fit on our thumbs.

I could've worn the ring on a chain around my neck, but I couldn't stand necklaces or anything around my neck.

"What happened to 'Hi, honey, how are you?'" I kissed my mom on top of her head.

She mumbled something in Korean and laughed. Sometimes I wished she'd taught me Korean, like she'd taught my children.

"We too busy for that, you know. Have too much of the work to do." Yunni waved her hands at me as if shooing away flies. "Go now. Get to work."

"This could be considered child abuse or could be breaking some sort of child labor law," I joked.

"You adult, no child. No law broke." She steered me into the back room. "Oh, and remember, I take girls to Korea soon, right?"

"That is still under discussion."

"Have tickets. All planned. They go like their brothers did at their age. Lots of family to see in my home country. Andrew and you come with, too. All worked out. You don't worry about that now. Go to do your job."

I unloaded a crate of organic fruits and vegetables. Then my eighty-eight-year-old paternal Welsh grandfather, who we called Tadcu, entered the room. "Hey, chickadee, don't you look like a peach today?"

"Thanks, Tadcu, you're looking mighty spiffy, too."

He wore a seersucker blazer over a white linen shirt and had on a navy-blue bow tie that matched his slacks. His white leather shoes were without a scuff mark. He had thick white hair and deep blue eyes. It'd nearly killed him to lose his only child, my father. I imagined that, had my dad lived, he'd have aged as gracefully as his father.

Tadcu now thought it was his responsibility to take care of Yunni and me.

"Are you going anywhere special today?" I pried a crate open using a screwdriver.

"I'm taking Miss Annie Mae out to lunch." He winked. "I hope I get lucky."

"Jeez, you men are all the same. One-track minds."

5

"Two-track mind. Rugby is the other one." He picked an apple from the crate I'd opened. "Better yet, if I can die while making love to a beautiful lady with rugby on the television in the bedroom, that would be heaven."

Picturing Tadcu making love, especially with Annie Mae—one of my closest friends—made my brain ache and eyes sting. But he'd been widowed over ten years, so I guessed he should be out there again dating. That still didn't prevent it from feeling weird.

I switched the topic. "Where are you taking her for lunch?"

"The DeSoto Hilton. They have a nice little lunch buffet." Tadcu pocketed the apple. "It's a hotel, too, so if things go well, we can get a room. I better grab something for protection."

"Please tell me you're getting an umbrella, since we've had so much rain, and not referring to anything else."

"Why, of course." Tadcu slid the closet door open and pulled out an umbrella. "I'm feeling lucky."

"Enough." I directed Tadcu out of the storeroom. I called out, half laughing, to my husband, "Can you please do something with him?"

"Not my turn," Andrew called back.

After Tadcu left, I called José, my police officer friend.

José answered his phone on the first ring. "Hey, Cat, what can I do for you?"

"You know I hate to bother you. But can you see if one of your new hires would consider reopening the case about that night?" I asked. "If there are new eyes on it, maybe they'll find something that everyone else missed. Please?"

"I'll see what I can do. Catch ya later tonight." He clicked off.

I'd only have closure and feel that my family was safe if the killer was behind bars. Making sure this happened became my mission.

CHAPTER 2

Six-foot, four-inch José strode into Bezu's dining room, the location for our meeting of the Chubby Chicks Club. José folded himself into a chair and then, without any greeting, said, "So I'm called to Ardsley Park because it's flooded again. This lady thinks that her dog, Pup Diddy, is still in her car parked in front of her house. All I saw in the water was the car's roof; I couldn't see in any windows. So, in my black wet suit, I dive under this murky, brown, debris-ridden filth, trying to smash the car window. After a few minutes, I emerge covered in Spanish moss and God knows what else, looking like the Creature from the Black Lagoon. Just then, the lady, who's standing on her porch, screams over to me, 'Pup Diddy is upstairs sleeping.' So I guess you can say my day as one of Savannah's finest went as usual."

Bezu shook her blond head and poured José a glass of iced tea. We all called her Bezu, which was short for Barbara Elizabeth Susan. "Y'all know that the flooding has been a problem for years. The city needs to take care of it once and for all."

"When pigs fly." Annie Mae, a sixty-five-year-old African-American woman, shoved her eyeglasses up on her short, wide nose. Her brown eyes twinkled behind the glass. Her round face then filled with a smile accentuated by full red lips. "The city is like Armstrong University. In the three decades I taught there, no one knew what change meant. Except for the extra coins in one's pocket."

"Maybe we don't want to adjust too much for fear of losing our Savannah charm," added Bezu, the Southern belle of the group.

"Lose something, that's for sure." José resembled, and often was mistaken for, the wrestler/actor Dwayne "The Rock" Johnson. José was a bomb squad detective who never had fewer than a dozen female admirers pining for his attention. They didn't stand a chance. José preferred males.

My cell buzzed, indicating a message. I read it. "Lucy's running a little late but will be here soon."

José sat up straight. "So, what's going on with the rest of you?"

Annie Mae stirred a packet of raw sugar into her tea. "Trying to keep out of trouble now that I've reduced my workload. I'm planning to retire soon, so I'm testing the waters to see what life will be like when I don't work anymore. If anyone's interested in joining me, I just started taking water aerobics at the aquatic center Monday and Wednesday mornings at eight."

"No water aerobics for me," José replied. "Gotta save the city."

"Me either," I said. "After the boys catch the bus, I take the girls to school, then help Andrew and my mom at the store. Otherwise, it sounds like fun. I enjoy taking classes when I have time. They keep me well-rounded."

"And I just loved the self-defense class we all met at a couple of years back. We need to do something like that again," Bezu said.

José pointed to his chest. "Next month I'm teaching another one, if you know anyone who might be interested."

"You taught me how to kick some butt, except I can barely move mine anymore. That's why I'm doing the water aerobics." Annie Mae patted her full figure and then reached for a chunk of cheese and a cracker from the doily-covered silver platter set in the middle of the dining room table. "Got to get in shape. I'm a little *too* well-rounded."

"Bless your heart, you always make me laugh," Bezu said to Annie Mae. "You really are the life of this little group."

"Group of misfits." José grinned.

"Misfits? That's why we didn't let you name the group. You'd come up with some lame name. Not as clever as mine: 'The Chubby Chicks Club.'" Annie Mae took a bite of cracker.

"Still don't get that, considering we're not all chicks, nor are we all chubby." José squeezed a lemon slice into his glass.

"Hey, I'm both chubby and a chick. Plus, I love the alliteration." Annie Mae took a sip of tea.

"Me too. I think our name is fun." I plopped a chunk of cheese into my mouth. "Although, maybe not so much the chubby part, since today a customer thought I was pregnant."

"Don't mind them. You look great. I can't imagine having children, let alone four like you did." Bezu glanced at her long, thin, manicured fingers.

We all gathered a few times a month around Bezu's dining room table in her three-story Georgian house on Forsyth Park. When General Oglethorpe founded the city of Savannah, Bezu's family, the Gordons, owned half of it. After the Great Depression, a recession, and some unlucky gambling, all that remained of the family fortune was the timeworn mansion.

In the center of the dining room sat a mahogany table with eight matching, high-back, carved chairs. An antique sideboard and a china cabinet were on opposite walls. The washed-out heart pine floors were covered with a thick, dark Oriental rug. From the twelve-foot ceiling, a dusty, three-tiered crystal chandelier hung over the center of the table.

"I love you all. I can't imagine not having you in my life. Especially after my dad…" I swallowed as I held back tears. My friends had brought me so much support and comfort after my dad was killed.

"Yes, darling, we've been together for good times and bad. Thankfully, way more good." Bezu reached over and held my hand.

Through the dining room window, the late-afternoon sun

shone on Bezu, making her blond hair and pale skin almost translucent. She smelled of rosewater.

"Here's to more good times." Annie Mae lifted her glass in a toast.

We all followed suit and clinked our glasses together.

Just then, the door opened, and a short, Asian man walked past the dining room, humming what sounded like the Bruno Mars's song "Locked out of Heaven." He made his way up the stairs.

José jumped out of his chair, his hand over the gun on his hip. "Do you know him?"

"Calm down." Bezu ran over to José. "Don't shoot the poor man."

José slowly sat down, still eyeing the stairwell.

"Who is he?" I asked Bezu.

"Um. He's a relative." Bezu looked at the ceiling. "Mr. Phong. He's visiting me for a spell."

"He doesn't look like any relative of yours," Annie Mae said. "I mean, your whole family is born and bred Deep South. He's Eastern. Far East."

Bezu fidgeted with her pearl necklace. "He's the brother-in-law of my second cousin twice removed."

"Why do you call him Mr. Phong?" José asked. "After all, he is a relative. Sort of."

Then we heard footsteps again, and Mr. Phong appeared in the doorway.

Bezu walked over to him and put her hand on his shoulder. "Mr. Phong, I'd like you to meet José, Annie Mae, and Cat. They are dear friends of mine."

"Hey, I just met you, and me is crazy, but call my number maybe." Mr. Phong smiled, showing crooked white teeth. His thin black hair fell on his slightly wrinkled forehead. I figured that he was in his late sixties. His brown tweed suit looked one size too big for him. He nodded his head like a bobblehead toy.

"What the heck?" Annie Mae looked appalled. "I'm not giving a stranger my number."

I interrupted Annie Mae. "Pleasure meeting you, Mr. Phong."

"Hey." José nodded his head toward Mr. Phong.

"Why does he want my number?" Annie Mae asked Bezu.

"He doesn't. He's learning English by listening to music. Mainly pop songs. That was sort of the lyrics to a Carly Rae Jepson song." Bezu quickly guided Mr. Phong to the door as he sang Lady Gaga's "Bad Romance."

When Bezu returned, Annie Mae said, "You sure have had a lot of relatives visit lately. And they stay such a long time."

"Everyone and anyone who is remotely related to me finds out I live in this gorgeous city and have a big house to stay in, and, well, you know how that goes." Bezu sat down.

"Humph." Annie Mae raised an eyebrow.

"So what's going on with your family, Cat?" José stretched his long legs and clasped his hands behind his head, showing off well-developed muscles.

"Before I forget, as part of their senior high school project, Timmy and Teddy want to job-shadow you. They think it'll be cool to hang around a cop all day." I shifted forward in my chair.

"I'll get that set up. I just need to clear it with my boss." José took a swig of tea. "I think they'll have a blast."

"I hope they don't, considering you work on the bomb squad." Annie Mae chortled.

"Yeah, no explosions. Promise, José? Or you'll have to answer to me." I hoped it sounded more like a demand than a request. As a forty-year-old mom, I looked exhausted all the time rather than formidable. I doubted anyone took me too seriously, least of all José.

He put his hands up. "No guarantees."

"Before I forget, how was your date with Tadcu? I mean, my grandfather," I asked Annie Mae.

"You had a date?" José high-fived Annie Mae.

"Not that I kiss and tell, but he's such a gentleman. And so romantic, too. He gave me an apple. Flowers are so passé." Annie Mae cleared her throat. "We had an absolutely lovely time. That's all I'm saying about that."

The door opened with a creak, and a gust of muggy air blew in as Lucy walked through the door. Her trademark red lipstick matched her flushed cheeks. "Gracious Almighty Lord. The humidity is killing me." She set a round glass container down on the table and removed the lid to reveal an apple pie.

We said our hellos as Lucy got situated. As usual, when we got together, we did a potluck. This time, Bezu had made a roast with vegetables, José had brought a tossed spring salad, Annie Mae had contributed macaroni and cheese, and I'd supplied two bottles of wine.

"Now that we're all here, let me see about dinner." Bezu rose.

"Let me help." Annie Mae followed Bezu into the kitchen.

José's cell phone rang. He excused himself and stepped outside, leaving Lucy and me together.

"You're not pregnant, are you?" Lucy asked.

"Huh?"

"There." Lucy motioned toward my midsection. "Muffin top or baby?"

"You're the second person today who thought that." That was it. Even though I'd changed my shirt, my pooch must have still been visible. Maybe I needed to lose a few pounds. At dinner, I'd load up on salad rather than pie, of which I already wanted two slices. "Not pregnant. Maybe a little muffin top."

"Thank goodness you're not, because you have the Noah's ark of uteruses. You'd end up with another set of twins on top of the two sets you already have. Speaking of the kids, school ends soon. Do they have plans for summer?" Lucy asked as she plopped into a chair.

"Nina and Nancy start a summer program at Savannah Children's Theater."

"I lost track, how old are they now?"

"Five."

"Wow. Time goes by quickly." Lucy shook her head. "And it's your boys' last year of high school, and then they're off to college."

"Don't remind me. I'm losing half my kids."

"You're not, really. I'm sure they'll come home a lot."

"I sure hope so."

"What are their summer plans?"

"They decided they didn't want to work at the family business. Instead, Timmy is working at Leonardo's ice cream shop, and Teddy cuts grass. They're pooling their money to get a car because they're under the impression that they're the only eighteen-year-olds in the universe who don't have one."

I paused before asking, "How is Bert's retirement going?"

Lucy poured herself a glass of tea, then took a linen napkin and dabbed at the perspiration on her forehead. "Right now, we're battling our backyard neighbors, the Nesmiths."

"About what?" I asked.

"Ina said that we cut the roots of the hackberry tree that borders our property. It was the plumber, not us, who cut them. Now she's afraid it'll die and fall on her house. The whole situation is a mess and getting very hostile." Lucy sighed and shrugged. "But it's better that he focus his energies on that than chasing me around the house."

"Chasing you?"

"Oh, yeah. I don't know what possessed him, but all of a sudden, he's working out and taking Viagra. After he pops one, I tell you what, it's hard getting away from him." Lucy raised an eyebrow and leaned in. "Really hard."

I felt myself blush. She wasn't afraid to say anything, and I liked that about her. "I wonder why he's doing all that."

"I'm not sure. Do you think he's having an affair? There was a credit charge at Levy's jewelers. Maybe it's a surprise gift for me?" Lucy turned her palms up. "Sometimes he disappears for hours at a time with no notice. Then other times, he's underfoot and very affectionate with me. Weird, huh?"

"Yeah." In the back of my mind, I did wonder about Bert cheating on Lucy, but pushed that thought out. After all, Bert was a paunchy, middle-aged, somewhat nerdy retired accountant. Not exactly playboy material.

"Anyway, his friend James Cohen owns a lake house in North Carolina. Bert is spending a few days there, so I know he'll just be with James and two other guys. Since he's out of my hair, I've redone my sitting room from top to bottom."

"One day I'd love for you to redo my master bedroom. I think it's been the same for twenty years. Kids, their toys, and fingerprints have been the only additions to the décor."

"I'd love to. Oh, and by the way, don't let me forget to give these to Annie Mae." Lucy pulled a paper bag from her purse and set it on the table. "She loves peaches, and the Red and White had a big sale on them."

"The Sunshine Market has peaches." I smiled.

"Of course, if I were on that side of town today, I would've gone to your store instead."

"I know. I'm just teasing you."

"And when I'm at the Red and White, the Blue Belle Antique Shoppe is just down the street, so I always stop in there, too. Just today, I found some great things."

"Like what?"

"A cute vase, which looks old, came in a grab-bag-type box called a mystery box. It's simply gorgeous and works perfectly with the new color scheme in the sitting room."

"What colors did you go with?"

"Modern cool colors with an eclectic touch." Lucy adjusted her magenta-rimmed glasses, which matched her billowy blouse. Her chestnut hair was twisted in a loose chignon bun, with a few strands of gray hanging around her face. "Here's a picture I took of the room this morning."

She turned her cell phone toward me. The walls were decorated with picture frames holding black-and-white photos. A white leather sofa with turquoise-and-tan throw pillows sat atop a block-print rug. A gorgeous blue-and-white vase with yellow roses, a stack of books, and a few other tasteful knick-knacks adorned the white, shabby chic square coffee table.

"Very artsy," I said.

"I'm telling you, after all these years decorating clients' homes, it sure is nice to finally have time to focus on my own." Lucy stirred Splenda into her iced tea.

"I bet." Then I noticed a large bandage wrapped around her right hand. "What happened?"

She put her phone back in her purse. "Burned myself taking out the pie. It's no big deal, really, other than now it's a little difficult to grab things with it. It's fine. I dabbed a little aloe on it."

"Good."

"Oh, before I forget, that same box with the vase ended up containing five adorable dinner plates. Anyway, one of the plates was wrapped in the newspaper crossword puzzle page. Some of the spaces were filled in with the words 'Your next' in purple ink. Y-O-U-R. This was not only misspelled, but also not the correct answer to fourteen down."

It felt like a metal wrecking ball had collided with my stomach. "Do you think the message was meant for you?"

"No way. I have no enemies. Besides, everything was already wrapped in the box before I even bought it. So it's not like anyone even knew that I'd be the one buying the box." Lucy shook her head. "Just saying, it may have nothing to do with that night, but I knew you'd want to know."

"Thanks." Was it pure coincidence or another clue to help solve my dad's murder? My gut twisted as a chill ran down my spine.

"I brought it here." Lucy pulled the paper out of her large quilted handbag and gave it to me. "Should we show José?"

I held the paper as though it were dusted with arsenic. It was dated a week ago. My insides flipped. Could the same person who'd killed my father have done the crossword?

As if on cue, José entered the room. "Sorry, I had to take that call."

We brought José up to speed on our conversation. I handed him the newspaper.

"Cat, I know why this worries you." José looked me in the eye. "I'll make a few calls and see what I can find out."

"Thanks." I felt my eyes well up.

José put his hand on my shoulder. "You know I'll help you for as long as it takes to find an answer that'll give you closure."

"You're a good man, José. Let me give you some sugar."

He leaned down to meet me and I gave him a peck on the cheek.

"Still doesn't do anything for me, but thanks." José smirked.

I pointed to the paper in his hand. "Maybe this is finally the break I need."

Lucy held up her tea glass. "Here's to you finding an answer, and here's to me finding ways to keep sane while Bert's retired."

"Cheers." I clinked my glass to hers.

Bezu entered the dining room, Annie Mae at her heels. "Pardon my interruption, but I'm afraid dinner is a little delayed. My oven has been acting up. I underestimated the time it takes to cook the vegetables. They still need about a half hour."

Annie Mae set down a glass bowl full of salad on the table. "Have some salad while we wait."

Bezu placed two bottles of dressing and wood tongs next to the salad.

"Before I forget, these are for you, Annie Mae." Lucy offered Annie Mae the bag of peaches.

"Thank you. You're always so thoughtful." Annie Mae held the bag. "I hope that you didn't go out of your way to get these."

"Nope," Lucy said.

"I've been busier than a moth in a mitten." Bezu began to pace. "I thought I had some fresh bread to serve with our meal, but I can't find it. I feel like the most incompetent hostess."

"I told her we don't need any bread, but you know how Bezu gets when she's stuck on a thought." Annie Mae turned up her hands.

"I have some fresh dinner rolls I just got today. Let me scamper home and get them." Lucy stood and slung her purse over her shoulder. "I'll be back in a few minutes. By then, supper will be ready."

"No, don't bother," Annie Mae said.

"Yes, please don't," Bezu added.

"I absolutely insist." Lucy walked to the door. "I'll be back before you know it."

Bezu gave in. "That is so very kind of you."

"I'll go with you," José offered.

"Me too," I put in.

Lucy held her keys in her hand. "No. No. Don't be silly. I'll be back in a flash." Lucy blew us air-kisses and left.

"What a sweetie, huh?" Bezu uncorked a bottle of red wine.

"She's one of a kind, that's for sure." I hoped that the crossword puzzle Lucy found was also one of a kind and not related to anyone else's death. Yet the hairs on my arms stood on end.

CHAPTER 3

*T*hirty minutes passed, and Lucy had not returned. We tried phoning her several times, but the calls went directly to her voice mail.

I looked at my cell. Still no missed calls or texts from Lucy. The crossword puzzle with purple ink really bothered me. Paranoia drenched my thoughts to the point where I had to do something. "I need to go to Lucy's house."

"Cat, she probably got caught up in something and forgot about the time." Annie Mae put her hand up. "And dinner is ready."

"I'm sure she'll be here any minute." Bezu fidgeted with her pearl necklace. "However, it's unlike Lucy not to answer her phone."

Looking out the window at Forsyth Park, I hoped to see Lucy heading up the walkway. A few joggers ran by, followed by a couple pushing a baby in a stroller. "I have to see what's going on and if she's okay."

Annie Mae huffed. "You're being fearful for no reason."

"Maybe." I turned on my heels. "But I'm going to her house."

"I'll come, too." José stood. "I need to stretch my legs anyway."

"What about dinner?" Annie Mae asked.

"It's not good manners to eat without everyone here. I'm joining y'all, too," Bezu said.

"You're going to find her in the middle of a project she got caught up in and lost track of time. You know how she sees something out of place, and next thing you know, she's redecorated the whole room." Annie Mae made a circular motion with her finger.

"If that's the case, then we can speed her along and get her back here so we can have dinner." I grabbed my purse, feeling a little sick to my stomach. I worried enough for a hundred people. Yet I didn't know how to stop my spiraling thoughts filled with doom.

"Fine, then. I'll go as well, since Bezu said we can't eat without Lucy." Annie Mae stood.

Bezu turned off the oven, and Annie Mae put the salad back in the refrigerator. José wrote a note and put it on the front door, just in case Lucy showed at the house.

The four of us walked along the tree-lined sidewalk in Forsyth Park toward Lucy's house. The hot air coated my skin in a thick blanket of moisture. Spanish moss hung like cotton candy from the live oaks on either side of the path. Draping tree branches provided a canopy of shade from the late-afternoon sun. We walked around puddles from recent rains.

"Why the hell did we decide to walk?" Annie Mae gasped for breath. "I sure as hell did not get my PhD and work all those years at the university to finally be near retirement only to die of heatstroke."

"Stop griping," José said to Annie Mae. "You're a woman of leisure now. How would you like to put your life on the line every day like I do?"

"What the hell has that got to do with anything?"

"Everything and nothing," José shot back, and grabbed Annie Mae around her waist. He gave her a big squeeze.

"You let go of me now." Annie Mae giggled. "I'm calling the police on you for aggravated assault."

"I *am* the police." José let her go as he playfully patted her arm.

"All right, you two, cut it out," I joked. "Jeez. My kids are better behaved."

"Which set? Your teen boys or the little girls?" Bezu asked me.

"Both." I tapped José on the arm. "Behave."

"I didn't get a chance to talk to Lucy before she left," Bezu said.

"Neither did I." Annie Mae smiled. "She sure is thoughtful. I can't wait to eat those peaches."

"Cat, you had time to chat with her. How is Bert's retirement going?" Bezu asked.

"I bet she finds any dang excuse she can to keep him out of her hair now that they're both retired," Annie Mae panted. "When I still had my Ernie, if he'd get underfoot, I'd send him to the hardware store to buy a little box of something. I have a whole garage packed full of nuts, bolts, and screws."

"As usual, she's busy decorating." I lifted the hair from my warm neck and pulled it into a ponytail. "She just redid her sitting room."

"Her taste is absolutely exquisite." Bezu fanned herself with her hand. "It's hotter than blue blazes. Thank goodness we've only got one more block."

"I feel like I'm melting." I wiped the perspiration from my forehead.

"Only the Wicked Witch melts," José said to Annie Mae. "Annie, baby, I'm going to miss you when you liquefy."

"Good one. I guess you have a brain cell in that straw head of yours." Annie Mae whacked José on the back with her purse.

"Assault!" José snatched Annie Mae's purse and put it on his arm. He swayed his hips, elbows at his side, forearms out front, and held his wrists limp. "I'm Annie Mae. I'm sassy and politically incorrect as hell."

"Stop. People are looking at us." Bezu advanced a few feet in front of the group.

Annie Mae shook her hands about. "Who cares? You could waste your whole life trying to please everyone. All that worrying you do about what people think about you and what you look like and all that nonsense. You're going to fret yourself into thin air."

"Take that from an expert. Annie doesn't please anyone." José handed Annie Mae her purse.

"Why should I? I've got you crazy people who irritate the wits out of me. That's all the aggravation I need." Annie Mae grinned.

"We love you, too." My insides spun into knots worrying about Lucy.

"Thank goodness we're here," Bezu said.

We followed Bezu up the steps to Lucy Valentine's house.

Bezu sighed. "Sometimes I'm embarrassed to be seen with you all out in public. Gracious, it's like a circus."

"And who doesn't love a circus?" I rang the bell. "Except for the creepy clowns—I hate adults dressed in costumes with their faces covered. It freaks me out."

No one answered the door. We stood in silence for a minute.

I tried calling Lucy again. The call went to voice mail. "Where is she?"

"Move your sorry white behinds aside." Annie Mae shouldered her way to the door. "This is how you get in." She banged at the door with her fists and yelled for Lucy. All of Savannah probably heard her. In fact, all of Georgia. Maybe South Carolina, too.

Still no answer.

"Apparently, Lucy is preoccupied, and we should use good manners and leave. Plus, I'm feeling a little faint from the heat and not eating." Bezu straightened her floral sundress around her waist. She retrieved a tissue from her purse and dabbed the perspiration from her forehead.

We stood on the porch of the two-story, yellow row house. The sweet aroma from a tea olive shrub nearby permeated the air.

I peered into the front picture window. "The lights are on, but I don't see her inside."

"I say we go in." Annie Mae looked through the glass panel in the door.

"Then we do it my way." José jiggled the doorknob. He took

something out of his pocket. I couldn't see what he was doing. His back was to me.

"That's a scary thought coming from a bomb guy," I said.

"Y'all are making me anxious." Bezu paced the porch.

"We're in." José opened the door. "Welcome, my ladies."

"That's called getting the job done." Annie Mae made her way into the house.

We all followed, entering the sitting room first.

I darted my eyes around, looking for Lucy.

"Y'all are absolute barbarians breaking in." Bezu strolled about Lucy's sitting area. "My oh my, it sure is nice and cool in here. Maybe I can get a beverage. I'm parched."

"Holy smokes. That's ugly." Annie Mae stood in front of the love seat in the sitting room. She pointed to what looked like a paint-it-yourself blue-and-white vase on the coffee table.

"I do declare. Not at all what I expected Lucy would ever purchase." Bezu leaned into the vase, forming her pink-lipsticked mouth into a pout.

"It looks like a monkey painted it." José walked around. "But I love everything else."

I shook my head. That vase had sure looked better in the picture Lucy had shown me earlier. The yellow roses in the vase seemed as though they had been shoved in haphazardly, as a few of the stems were bent over, the flowers scattered on the table. Lucy was a neatnik, so I was surprised she'd leave anything lying around. I picked up the petals and put them in my purse to throw away later.

Annie Mae yelled, "Lucy!"

We began to walk down the wood-floored hallway, four sets of shoes clopping to the back of the house.

Bezu entered the kitchen first.

"Lucy," I shouted.

"Lucy, I'm home!" José screamed like Ricky Ricardo had done on the *I Love Lucy* show.

"Okay. I'm seriously worried now." My chest tightened.

"Me too." Bezu opened a closet door.

"Where is she?" Annie Mae poked her head into a walk-in closet.

"José, please call your people at the police department." I ran into another room, looking for Lucy. "Remember the crossword puzzle?"

"Everyone calm down," José shouted. "Let's search every room first."

José and Annie Mae looked upstairs. Bezu and I explored the main level. The rooms were very much in order. A cross hung in every room. Fresh flowers sat in vases throughout the house. But it didn't appear that anyone was home. Even though there were shoes near the front door, a sweater thrown over a chair, and dishes in the sink. My heart raced, and my hands began to shake.

I had this ominous feeling that something was wrong.

Really wrong.

We met back downstairs in the kitchen.

"Look here." José held the pantry door open and pointed at Lucy's purse next to a clear bakery bag of dinner rolls on a shelf. He picked up the bag of rolls. "They're already cut in half, too."

On the counter next to the sink sat a cutting board scattered with crumbs. A serrated knife lay near a knife block set—which had two slots empty.

Rocks formed in my gut. "This is not good."

José dialed Lucy's cell. We heard ringing coming from the pantry.

I ran in and picked up Lucy's purse. Pulling out her phone, my hands shook. "Call the police now."

"Hold on, Cat. Maybe a neighbor came by, and she got to chatting with them." José went over to a window and pulled the curtains back.

"Maybe, but it may not have been a social call. They're fighting with one neighbor, Ina Nesmith, over tree roots." I began to pace the kitchen floor, its red-accented white tiles matching the red-and-white checkered cloth on the table.

"What are you implying?" José asked.

23

"Things are not right." I glanced around the kitchen. Nothing seemed out of place. Yet everything felt askew.

"Have you tried that back door?" Annie Mae pointed to the closed door near the rear of the kitchen that lead to a mudroom.

"I'll check it out." José strode to the back.

He turned the handle and swung open the door.

Lucy lay on her back on the lime-green linoleum floor, dark red blood pooled around her left arm. Her wrist was slit open. A butcher knife lay near her right hand.

I screamed.

"Holy smokes," Annie Mae said.

"Oh, my." The color drained from Bezu's face as she leaned against the kitchen table.

My knees buckled under me. I felt the contents of my stomach lurch into the back of my throat.

CHAPTER 4

*J*osé checked Lucy's vital signs. "She's dead."

I knelt down and held Lucy's cool hand. My heart raced, and my stomach flipped. Had the crossword killer struck again? No. Lucy had said that the paper was already in the box before she'd purchased it. It couldn't be the same killer, could it?

José grabbed a kitchen towel and used it to pick up a folded piece of white paper. "There's a note."

"What does it say?" Annie Mae asked.

José opened the paper. "One side is from someone named Ina Nesmith. That's her neighbor you mentioned, isn't it, Cat?"

I nodded.

José continued. "It says, 'Back off, Lucy, or else. —Ina.' The other side, written in what looks like pink lipstick, reads, 'It's over. Lucy.'" José put the note back on the floor where he had found it. "This appears to be a possible suicide note. But then again, Ina's note could be construed as a threat. Either way, no one touch anything. This is now a crime scene."

"Why would she kill herself? She was happier than a pig in mud." Bezu sat down in a chair as she pressed her trembling hand to her chest.

"Hell if I know." Annie Mae pulled a chair next to Bezu at the kitchen table. She reached over and held Bezu's hand.

"I'm calling my precinct right now." José held his phone to his head.

I paced the floor as though my legs couldn't stand still. Filling the room with a floral scent, so light and alive, was a vase of fresh-cut flowers sitting in the middle of the kitchen table.

"Lucy had been gone less than two shakes of a lamb's tail. How could this happen?" Bezu rocked herself.

José held a hand up. "Everyone sit tight. Help is on the way."

I wiped tears with the back of my hand. My taste buds flooded with sour bile. I tensed with raw nerves as a chill ran down my spine. And yet, I felt numb.

A short while later, two squad cars and an ambulance arrived. For the next few hours, the house buzzed with activity. Police forensic officers and EMTs began doing their work. José talked with them as they took pictures, dusted for prints, secured the area, filled out reports, walked through the house, and strung up yellow tape. We were all interviewed as witnesses. Bezu, Annie Mae, and I sobbed the whole time.

After I composed myself, I walked to José just as a detective approached him.

The detective, with a name badge reading Ray Murphy, pointed a thick finger at José. "This is my case. Back off."

"Listen here, Ray. The vic is my friend. It's not suicide." José shook his head. "I'd just seen her right before she left to grab dinner rolls. She was fine. And what about the note that was left? You need to interview Ina Nesmith."

"Don't tell me how to do my job." Ray stood face to face with José and poked him in the chest. Ray stood an inch shorter than José but had a stout, thick build and a blond crew cut. "This is my case."

José's neck flushed as he leaned toward him. "Then do this by the book. No shortcuts."

"You're not my boss. Scarcely my peer." Officer Ray didn't budge. "A suicide note, a knife in the vic's hand. I think this case will be closed by the time the ink dries on the report."

José stayed face to face with Ray. "You have a problem with me, fine. But keep your beef with me out of this case."

Ray chortled. "The dying for dinner rolls case is cut-and-dried. Case closed."

José leaned in. His hands formed into fists. His neck veins bulged.

Ray took a step back. "One day, I'll have proof of who you are, and your ass will be fired."

"If you have something on me, then do something about it. If not, get off my back." José narrowed his eyes.

"I don't have anything concrete now. But I will. There is something you're doing that is a disgrace to the department, and when I find out, I'll expose you." Ray clenched his jaw.

"You're out of line. You have nothing on me because I've done nothing wrong. You hate me, and that's fine. But don't let that obstruct this investigation." José jutted his chin. "If you're still pissed I won at poker, I can give your money back if that'll make you stop bitching."

"Shove it." Ray turned and shouted over his shoulder, "All of you need to get out of the house now."

"Jackass," José said under his breath as we exited the house.

We made our way out to the front yard.

"What about Lucy's husband?" Bezu asked. "Did anyone call him?"

"He's been notified and is on his way now," José said.

"I can't believe this happened." I rubbed my forehead.

"I feel frozen, like I can't think right," Annie Mae added.

"Me too," Bezu said.

"It's because you all are in shock. It's difficult to process right away." José put on his dark aviator sunglasses.

We stood in silence on Lucy's front lawn. It was dusk. The smell of fresh-cut grass permeated the air. A slight breeze moved branches of the oak tree above us. The air hung heavy with the remnants of the humid, hot day.

Each of us seemed lost in our own thoughts. I kept going over the last few times that I'd seen Lucy. Her energy, her talkative nature.

Hearing footsteps, I turned toward the front door.

A jet-black body bag on a stretcher was being carried out by two EMTs.

My stomach wrenched, and my legs felt wobbly.

"Why would she do this?" Annie Mae sniffed and then blew her nose into a tissue.

Tears stung my eyes. "She wouldn't. My gut is saying that someone took Lucy's life."

"That's messed up." Annie Mae thumped her fist in the air.

I bit my lip. "This may be the same person who shot my dad. Lucy had found a crossword puzzle like the one found by my dad that night. Although she did say that it had already been in the box before she bought it."

"You think there's something there?" Annie Mae asked me.

"Y'all are making me nervous as a long-tailed cat in a room full of rocking chairs, talking about murder and a killer. No. No." Bezu pointed to her head. "She must've had some serious issues we didn't know about."

"Mental ones? I don't think so. She told us everything. Hell, half the time, I didn't want to hear every little detail of her personal business, but that's what she was like. So why wouldn't she have told us she was depressed? Enough to do this?" Annie Mae pantomimed a knife at her wrists.

"She didn't." I took a deep breath. "That suicide note was too brief for Lucy. Plus, she'd burnt her right hand and told me it was hard to grip things. So the whole knife thing doesn't sit right with me. And the threatening note from her neighbor is suspect, too. And did you notice that the lipstick on the note was pink, not Lucy's signature red color?"

"Those are some great observations." Annie Mae cocked her head as she looked at me. "So you're still thinking—"

"Someone killed her." I glanced at the half dozen potted flower arrangements alongside the front porch. There was water on the ground near them. "Everything in her house is so neat and in order. And look at how beautiful she keeps the place."

"And?" Annie Mae raised an eyebrow.

"The cat has food in his dish. These plants are freshly watered. This is all normal, routine-type stuff. Not a person on the edge, about to kill herself, right?" A tear streaked down my cheek. "She loved her cat, actually all animals. For the past fifteen years, she volunteered at the humane society. She would never do this, desert her cat. He was her child."

José held up a finger. "Except I've worked on many suicide cases. It's eerie how they get things in order just before they end their lives. So, it does seem that all outward evidence indicates suicide. But I agree she wasn't the type. She had lots of friends and hobbies and was very involved in her church. This doesn't sit right with me, either."

"Her poor husband. Bless his heart. He's got a tough row to hoe." Bezu dabbed her eyes.

"I'm not even going to ask what you just said. But as for Bert, I bet he killed her. It's usually the spouse that knocks off the other spouse." Annie Mae waved her hands. "Trust me, if Ernie's diet of Krispy Kreme hadn't killed him, I would've."

"You're all talk. You adored Ernie. If you ask me, he was a saint for putting up with you." José winked at Annie Mae.

Annie Mae tilted her head and grinned. "What fool thing are you talking about? My Ernie was the most stubborn man who ever walked the earth. Still, it seems that when a wife is killed, the husband did it."

"Not this time," José said. "I spoke to Lucy's husband. He's been on a fishing trip in North Carolina with his friends, so he has an airtight alibi."

Bezu wrung her delicate hands. "Why are we even discussing this? The law enforcement of this fine city will take care of it."

"Actually, ladies, we've been so overworked, even with a couple new hires, we are still understaffed. I've also been informed that this case will be wrapped up as suicide and closed before the end of the day." José wiped his brow.

"My tax dollars hard at work." Annie Mae rolled her eyes.

"Lord Almighty. Poor Lucy." Bezu threw her shoulders back and patted her blond hair, as if fixing herself up.

"Listen. There's something very wrong here, and we need to find out what." I choked on the words. "There may be a connection to my father's death."

"Cat, don't you have too much going on taking care of your children and your business to involve yourself in what is clearly police business and not ours?" Bezu asked.

"Cat's making some good points. I have to agree with her. Lucy's death doesn't feel right to me, either. And maybe José is right—which, by the way, would be a first." Annie Mae put on a half grin and turned to José.

"If it wasn't suicide, which it seems most of us agree it wasn't, then we have a much bigger issue, don't we?" I looked at each of them one by one. The words caught in my throat as my eyes teared up again. "Who killed Lucy?"

CHAPTER 5

*J*osé plopped in a chair. "Lucy's case has been closed as a suicide. The official investigation said she slit her left wrist with a butcher knife, lost a lot of blood, then fell and hit her head against the wall. There was a contusion on the back of her head."

We sat around Bezu's dining room table, having called a Chubby Chicks Club meeting. This was the first time we'd seen each other since Lucy's wake and funeral last week.

"Well, then, I think we forget any thoughts about it being anything other than what the police said it was." Bezu set a pitcher of iced tea on the table next to a large, red ceramic pot of shrimp jambalaya.

"Bezu, I disagree. I still think someone killed her." I unfolded the cream linen-and-lace napkin and set it on my lap. "As her friends, it's our duty to find out who did it. There's a possibility that her death may be connected to my dad's."

"Do you really think so?" Annie Mae asked.

"Maybe. Maybe not." I fought back a tear. "Regardless, Lucy is dead, and how it happened is suspicious. Like the mystery around my dad's murder."

"I'm with Cat." José scooped out jambalaya onto a plate. "It doesn't ring true to me, either. But my hands are tied. It's not my case."

"Why don't we do the investigation?" I took the plate José handed me.

"No." Bezu straightened her back.

"Maybe we should just drop it. Let Lucy rest in peace. Poor soul." Annie Mae made the sign of the cross. "Sorry, I still have leftover habits from twelve years of Catholic school. Praise the Lord. Let's eat."

"Now someone here is finally talking sense." Bezu took her fork. "José, thank you for serving. Now, why don't we chat about something more pleasant?"

"Annie Mae, I'm surprised you don't want to investigate it," I said.

"I'm educated in theater and the arts, not detective work." Annie Mae put a forkful of food into her mouth. "Plus, the police said it was suicide. And they're professionals. So maybe we should just agree with their expertise."

"Do you think they're right?" I asked.

Annie Mae nodded and then shrugged her shoulders.

I straightened my back. "I bet they didn't even follow up with the other side of the note, where Ina threatened Lucy. Or what about the lipstick on the note? That was not Lucy's color. Oh, and Lucy thought that Bert might have had a mistress, too. And I bet none of those leads were explored."

"They were not." José wiped his mouth with a napkin.

"So, you see, we need to examine possible suspects, at the very least." I looked around at each of them. "Who's with me?"

Annie Mae chewed and then swallowed.

Bezu looked down at the table.

"We need to find out how she died because she was our friend. And we are the only ones who can make this right." I slapped my hand on the table, hoping to get someone to react. It worked at the dinner table when my kids argued and caused a ruckus.

José laid the serving spoon on a plate. "I say we don't do anything."

"That's a good idea," Annie Mae agreed. "Let's leave it alone."

"Annie, that is a fine idea." José winked at Annie Mae.

"I say we don't leave it alone." I cut my eyes to José.

The spicy smell of the jambalaya lingered in the air.

José shook his head and looked away from me.

"Let's listen to José and drop it." Bezu glanced at me and smiled. "If you can't run with the big dogs, stay under the porch."

"What the heck? Bezu, please translate that from Southern to English," Annie Mae said.

"We don't have the law enforcement know-how, so we should stay out of any type of investigation." Bezu held Annie Mae's hand. "Can't we just talk about the festival next week?"

"While a dear friend of ours is dead? I can't think of anything else, festivals or otherwise." I pushed my plate away. "C'mon. The note from Ina, the pink lipstick, Lucy's happy disposition. There is so much that is not clear-cut. If any one of you can say for one hundred percent sure that it was suicide, then fine, you're out. But if you even have the slightest doubt, then it's your duty to find what really happened. We owe that to her."

José put his hands in the air, as if saying he gave up.

Bezu took a deep breath.

Annie Mae held her thumb and index finger a short distance apart. "I have a smidgen of doubt. So it wouldn't hurt to look into it just a little. Plus, I do have some free time now."

"Great, Annie Mae. I'm glad that at least someone else besides me can see that we need to do something."

"C'mon, José and Bezu," Annie Mae said. "The more I think about it, Cat's right. Someone killed our friend, and I want to know who and why. And put them behind bars for life."

"All in favor of looking into Lucy's death, say aye." I took a quick look around the room. The afternoon sun shone through the tall windows.

"Aye." Annie Mae fidgeted with a napkin.

José checked his cell phone, and Bezu fixated on a spot on the table.

Silence hung in the air.

Bezu sighed.

"I'm out." José stretched his long legs. "I'll say it once more. It's not my case. If I got involved, it'd be insubordination."

I held my hand up. "I move for the Chubby Chicks Club to accept this mission, even without José."

"Not a good idea." José shook his head.

"Jeez." Annie Mae glared at José. "Are you kidding me? You're not going to help us?"

"No. I have a bad feeling this is going to be a train wreck." José rolled his head side to side as if working out a crick in his neck. He stretched his arms, held out his hands, and cracked his knuckles. "And I don't want to get fired. I also think you should stay out of it."

"Fine. You're out, José," I said. "But I think the rest of us should investigate." I raised two fingers. "So far it's Annie Mae and me."

Annie Mae nodded and took another bite.

"What about you, Bezu?" I asked.

Bezu let out a deep breath. "Sorry, no. I think y'all even thinking about investigating Lucy's death with no experience is like having only one oar in the water."

"That means no, right?" Annie Mae said.

"Yes, it means no."

"So that just leaves Cat and me." Annie Mae's face twisted into a grimace. "What could go wrong?"

"Don't be so pessimistic," I told her. "It's our duty as Lucy's friends to do this for her."

"Right. Let's find her killer," Annie Mae agreed.

José took in a deep breath and then exhaled. "Since you're insisting on continuing with this, which I strongly advise you not to, then I can be an unofficial consultant. Just to keep you two out of jail. But that's it."

"Thanks, José. Any help from you is better than none." Annie Mae's face softened. "And don't you think it was weird the way Lucy's husband was flirting at her wake? He practically jumped the bones of that redhead."

"Talk about inappropriate conduct." Bezu sighed. "He should be ashamed of himself."

"I saw that, too," José said. "Some folks use wakes as pickup places."

"Not us black folk. No, we honor the dead. We cry and carry on for days on end." Annie Mae thumped her chest.

I steered the conversation back on topic. "Maybe that was his mistress. Lucy had thought he might've been having an affair. Here's what I think we need to do next. I think we need to interview some people who knew her and find out if she had any issues or problems with anyone."

"Like someone who may have wanted her dead," Annie Mae added.

"Yes." I put my napkin on my plate.

"Great. The Chubby Chicks Club goes from misfit social group to amateur Southern sleuths. Well, at least half of the group." Annie Mae chuckled. "How in the hell did I get involved with this bunch of oddballs?"

"We needed an African American to round out the group." José playfully tapped Annie Mae on the arm. "And you were round."

"Just a little chubby." Annie Mae smiled. "You caught me at a vulnerable time, that's all. My Ernie had just died, so I wasn't in my right mind. Now I'm sort of attached to you all. Kind of like when you fall in love with a homely puppy no one wants."

Annie Mae and I came up with a few strategies to tackle Lucy's investigation. José listened and offered suggestions.

Annie Mae and I wanted to talk to Lucy's neighbor, Ina Nesmith, about the fight they'd had and the threatening note. I also thought that it was important to find out if Bert was having an affair and, if so, with whom. We also needed to somehow find out why Lucy's note had been written in pink lipstick and whose lipstick it could've been. Annie Mae planned to make a few phone calls, including some to Lucy's friends in her Bible study group.

Anne Mae and I intended to stop in at Lucy's favorite stores, the Red and White grocery and Blue Belle Antique Shoppe, in order to find out anything we could about her state of mind and if anything had seemed amiss in her life.

One thought kept nudging me: either there were two killers on the loose in Savannah, or just one. Could the same person have killed both my father and Lucy?

I shuddered. I abhorred either situation.

CHAPTER 6

*T*he next morning, I felt groggy. I'd tossed and turned all night thinking about Lucy.

Since it was Saturday, my eighteen-year-old sons, Teddy and Timothy, left early in the morning for their jobs. We lived in the Victorian District, close to downtown, so they either skateboarded or rode their bikes to work.

At my husband's and mom's insistence, I was taking a day or two off from the store. They had not been thrilled when I'd told them that Annie Mae and I were launching an investigation into Lucy's death. But they supported me and knew I was too stubborn and would do what I felt needed to be done.

My five-year-old daughters, Nina and Nancy, were spending the weekend at my sister-in-law's beach house on Tybee. I packed their beach gear and overnight bags before slathering sunscreen and kisses on them.

After dropping off the girls, I picked up Annie Mae, and we grabbed a cup of coffee at a drive-through while we planned our day.

Annie Mae sipped her coffee. "Whoa. Bitter. Needs way more sugar and a few more creamers. Hey, I forgot to tell you, I'm going to be a guest professor at UNC Chapel Hill. They have a great actor-training program and have asked me to help out."

A sadness overcame me. "North Carolina?"

"What's going on, Cat? You look like you lost your best friend."

"My mom told me she's taking the girls to Korea, and now you're leaving." I swallowed hard. "I'm feeling out of sorts, like something bad will happen if everyone leaves."

"Now listen here, Cat. Keeping people under your nose is not going to prevent anything bad happening to them. Didn't you tell me that your parents took the boys to Korea when they were five?"

"Yes."

"And they had a great time, right?"

I nodded. "But that was another time. Things have changed now. It's all different."

Annie Mae placed her hand on my shoulder. "No, it's not. What's happening here, I think, is that you are still blaming yourself for your father's death. And you are transferring all of that guilt and overprotecting those close to you."

"Wow, that was deep." I grinned.

"I minored in psychology."

"So where to now?" I drove my silver SUV. The air conditioner blasted, blending the smell of our fresh coffee with the bubble gum air freshener chosen by my girls.

"I've been thinking about this for a while. Bert killed Lucy. I just know it." Annie Mae poured a few sugar packets into her coffee and stirred with a red plastic stick.

"He has an alibi. Fishing at James Cohen's lake home in North Carolina."

"Yeah, right. But still I think we should double-check Bert's story. It's fishy."

I chuckled. "Why?"

"I don't know, but the way he was flirting with that redhead at Lucy's wake It's just not right. Something is going on with him that we need to figure out."

I drove east on DeRenne Avenue. "Lucy told me Bert was taking Viagra. She suspected that he had a lover."

"Let's go to James's house. I'm looking it up right now." Anne Mae tapped on her iPhone. "Take a left on Bull Street."

"What do we say to him?" I merged into the left lane. "I don't want to sound rude or nosy."

"Let me handle it." Annie Mae dumped three creamers into her coffee.

Several minutes later, we pulled in front of our destination, parked, and climbed out.

"Ready?" Annie Mae asked. "I'm all tingly and jittery. Probably because of all the excitement about sleuthing."

"I think it's from all the sugar you had. My kids get that way, too."

We walked in the sunny, muggy morning. The eighty-degree heat promised a blistering afternoon. I felt my skin frying as my hair clung to the back of my neck.

Annie Mae pushed the door buzzer.

The green door opened, and a bald man with tiny eyes and a hunched back greeted us. He looked like a mole. "What are you ladies selling?"

"Nothing. We're friends of Lucy Valentine." I stuck out my hand. "I'm Cat Thomson, and this is Annie Mae Maple."

"I think I remember seeing you two at Lucy's funeral last week." James shook our hands. He led us into his house. Smelling of beer and mothballs, the living room was dark, cool, and decorated with fishing memorabilia. A stuffed fish sat on a hallway table.

I began with, "I'm really sorry about disturbing you, but we wanted to—"

Annie Mae interrupted. "Find a liar."

James's mouth fell open for a second.

I shot Annie Mae a look that I hoped said "behave." "What Annie Mae means is that we loved Lucy and want some closure about what happened to her."

"She killed herself." James walked into a sitting room. We followed.

"Whoa. Listen here, Jimmy." Annie Mae got in his face. "That's our friend you're talking about. Please show some respect."

"Sorry. And it's James." He moved away from Annie Mae and

stood looking at fishing trophies on the fireplace mantel. "I don't know what I can do to help, but I have a few minutes. What do you need?"

Annie Mae picked up a trophy. "Well, it would be nice if you could tell us about the fishing trip you were on the day Lucy died."

"Um, yes. The trip." James studied his thumbnail. "We were up at my lake house in North Carolina."

"Who went with you on the trip?" I asked.

"Two buddies." James looked at the back of his hand.

I remember Lucy saying Bert went with three of his friends, so that would mean a total of four. James now said it was only two plus him. Three. "Who were they?"

"Smitty and Guy," James said.

"No one else?" I asked.

"Nah." James cracked his knuckles.

I got right in front of him, eye to eye. My kids could not lie if I looked them in the eye. "No Bert?"

James ran his finger along the edge of the mantel. "I mean there were, uh, four of us, including me and Bert, of course. I forgot to add Bert."

"First place, huh?" Annie Mae read the trophy in her hand. "James, you're quite the sportsman."

"And I got another first place a week ago." James picked up a folded newspaper on the end table and handed it to me.

It was the last page of the *North Carolina Times* sports section, dated a week ago. Two guys I didn't recognize wore fishing vests and wader pants. They must have been Smitty and Guy. They stood next to a grinning James, who held a fish by its tail. The picture credit read "Rex Mallard, Staff Photographer." Annie Mae looked over my shoulder at the picture.

"That's a huge fish," I said to James.

He puffed his chest out. "My biggest trout yet."

"Good job, James. That's a great catch." Annie Mae tapped the paper. "But where's Bert? I don't see him in the photo with you and your other two friends."

"Oh? Um. He…he took the picture," James mumbled.

"He didn't take this picture. The photo credit says Rex Mallard did," I added.

A fine sweat formed on James's nearly hairless head. His upper lip quivered. He grabbed the paper out of my hands and then took the trophy from Annie Mae. "Time to leave, ladies."

"Bert wasn't with you, was he?" I stared him down.

James broke eye contact with me and walked out of the room into the front foyer. "I don't have to talk to you and answer your stupid questions anymore, ladies. And I think our time here is done."

"Please, James, we really need your help," I said.

James looked away. "I'm sure you do. But I don't have to answer any more of your questions. I was trying to be nice, but now you are starting to irritate me."

"We really didn't mean to. We just wanted some help in finding answers." My eyes welled up.

"James, you seem like a good guy. I know you want to cooperate." Annie Mae trailed after James. "Please help us out here. My friend is sad. Can't you see her tears? Our hearts are broken over Lucy. We have to get some answers."

"I've told you all I could. You need to move your fat behind out of the way." James brushed his shoulder against Annie Mae.

"Whoa, now. That was below the belt. I may be a little chubby, but not fat." Annie Mae waved a hand up and down her body. "I think it all fits nicely together."

James rolled his eyes.

"James, we really don't want any trouble. We tried being nice to you, but apparently you don't want to be nice to us. So now I have to be firmer with you." Annie Mae moved closer to James. "Although I may look meek and mild, you need to know that I took a self-defense course. So I know some moves in case you push me again."

"Sorry about that. You were blocking my way," James said.

"Forgiven. Why don't you show your remorse by giving us some answers? 'Cause someone is fibbing here, and it isn't me," Annie Mae argued.

James turned his back to us. A light above him illuminated

the top of his head like a halo. "He's my friend. I can't throw him under the bus."

"I get that. I'm a mom of four kids, and I always tell them to be loyal to their friends. But this is different, James. This is murder." I gently placed a hand on his shoulder. "And I know you don't want to be an accomplice to the crime by lying."

"Murder?" James's voice rose as he turned to face us. "You think he killed his own wife?"

"Hell yes," Annie Mae said.

James swallowed. "No. He wouldn't do that."

I had to appeal to his sense of justice. "Whoever murdered Lucy may have also killed my father two months ago."

"Your family owns Sunshine Market. I remember reading about that. A burglary, right?" James looked at me.

"Not really, but that's not the point here." I caught my breath. "We need to know where Bert was when Lucy was killed. You were his alibi, and now that appears to be falling apart."

"I promised. I can't…" James looked like he wanted to cry, his face twisted, his eyes red.

"Okay. We get that. So how about you tell us without telling us? Let's use signals." I thought of a ploy I used on my kids to make them tell the truth without actually saying anything against someone else. "How about you tap your foot if Bert was with you, and touch your chest if he wasn't?"

"I like these signals." Annie Mae's words tumbled out. "Even better, why doesn't he blink twice if Bert was not with him and fold his arms if Bert was?"

James cleared his throat.

"What was that signal? Does that mean yes or no? Or maybe? We didn't have a maybe signal." Annie Mae arched an eyebrow.

James coughed, holding a fist to his mouth. "I had a tickle in my throat."

"This has gotten way too confusing." I sighed.

James blinked a couple of times.

"Are you flirting with me?" Annie Mae asked.

"No. I was giving you a signal," James explained.

"What did winks mean? I lost track of our codes," I said.

James sneezed.

Annie Mae shook a finger at him. "What does a sneeze mean?"

"I have allergies." He sniffed. "You two are driving me nuts."

"Fine. Let's start over," I said. "We'll get out of here if you just tell us the truth. And you won't even have to rat your friend out. Let's make it simple. Nod for yes, shake side to side for no, okay?"

Annie Mae stood next to James.

I continued, "Last week, when Lucy was killed, was Bert with you in North Carolina on a fishing trip?"

James shook his head from side to side.

CHAPTER 7

*A*fter leaving James and stopping at Krispy Kreme to fulfill Annie Mae's craving for a hot donut and cold chocolate milk, we made our way to Bert and Lucy's after navigating Saturday traffic.

Soon we pulled in front of their house. Annie Mae got out of the car. "I'm feeling really excited and tingly about all this."

"Sounds like another sugar rush." Slinging my purse over one shoulder, I saw Bert's yellow Mini Cooper with the black racing stripes. "Looks like Bert's here. Ready?"

"Yes." Annie Mae closed the door. "Let's get the fraud."

"Or at least find out where he was when Lucy was killed. That would help us decide if he's a suspect or not." With Annie Mae at my heels, I marched to the front door and rang the bell.

Bert opened the door after the fourth ring. "What are you two doing here?"

"Hi to you, too." Annie Mae glowered at Bert.

Bert's wet hair clung to his round head. He wore a pressed short-sleeved cotton shirt over his protruding belly and khaki shorts that showed his white, hairy legs. A fruity scent assaulted me. It must have been Bert's shampoo.

Bert ran a hand through his hair. "What do you gals need?"

"Nothing but the truth," Annie Mae said.

"I'm not sure what you're talking about." Bert stood in the

doorway, neither letting us in nor coming onto the porch with us.

"Let me try to explain. There are some things that are not adding up. As you know, my dad was killed, and now Lucy is also dead. I'm thinking that somehow their deaths may be related, although I'm not sure. That's why we are here," I told him.

"Is that so?" Bert smoothed his hair. "I'm still not getting what you want from me."

"I'd just like to clear up a few things," I said. "Ask you some questions, if that is okay with you?"

"Humph." Bert shifted from his right to his left foot.

"Where were you when Lucy died?" I asked.

"Uh, well, I don't know if I will answer that." Bert placed his hand on the doorknob.

"Please? I need to know." I tilted my head.

"Listen, ladies, you interrupted something important." Bert began to close the door.

Annie Mae stuck her foot in the way. "Hold on. We know your alibi stinks like a big old dead fish. So please answer Cat. It's really important."

Bert held the doorknob. He didn't make eye contact.

"Listen, Bert. You have to help us help you. Because right now I can call my friend at the police department and tell him that you were not where you said you were when Lucy died." I gave him my practiced pleading look, which included a sweet smile and a slight sideways glance.

Annie Mae wagged a finger at Bert. "Bert, I know we are all grieving here over Lucy. Because of that, we sometimes don't act like ourselves."

"And?" Bert asked.

"Emotions can run hot. I know I have been cranky and upset. But we all have to work through our grief. Some of us, like Cat and me, have too many unanswered questions about your wife's death. And because we loved Lucy, we need to find out what happened to her. It will give us closure on her death. We need to do this for our own sake," Annie Mae explained.

"What happened to her?" Bert said. "Everyone knows that she committed suicide. The police even said so."

"Do you believe she did that?" Annie Mae asked.

"Whether I believe it or not, that doesn't matter. It's what happened." Bert's eyes watered.

"That's what most people believe, but not us. We think someone may have killed her." I placed a hand on Bert's shoulder.

"You do? Why?" Bert looked at me.

"I'm not sure yet. That's why we are talking to you. We need some answers." I removed my hand.

"Could you please help us out here? I'm getting a little shaky standing in this heat," Annie Mae said to Bert.

"She's sugared up," I added.

"Huh?" Bert asked.

"It's a sugar and caffeine overload. I'm fit to be tied. I'm just saying that it's not a good combination," Annie Mae said. "I think I need some real food soon. But that's not important. What I need right now is for you to please tell us the truth."

"About what?" Bert said.

"Where were you the night Lucy died?" Annie Mae asked.

"Not that I need to tell you, but I was fishing."

"Oh no, you were not. I'm calling you out. We got it from a reliable source that you were not fishing. Bert, why aren't you telling us the truth?" Annie Mae shook her head. "Please don't insult our intelligence."

"It is the truth. I was at my friend James's lake home in the North Carolina mountains." Bert looked down at the ground.

"That's a tall tale for sure." Annie Mae leaned into the door next to Bert. "You need to level with us. A good start would be to be honest."

I implored, "Give us a straight answer. You don't want your name tied to two murders, do you?"

"Two murders?" Bert stammered.

"Lucy's and my dad's." My heart sank as I thought of them.

"Whoa, now. You're going off the deep end." Bert waved his hand. "I didn't kill anyone. Let alone two people."

Annie Mae dabbed her damp forehead. "It's so hot out here. Why don't you invite us in?"

"Um, I…I…can't," Bert stuttered. "I'm a little occupied right now. Could you come back later?"

Annie Mae folded her arms. "We'll leave as soon as you answer us. And if you don't, we'll just camp out here all night. You may need to get us a fan and maybe a chair and some cold drinks."

I stared him down. "Please, Bert. We think Lucy was killed, and since we found out that your fishing alibi fell apart, you may be considered a suspect."

"Unless you can tell us where you were," Annie Mae added.

Bert wiped a bead of perspiration from the top of his lip.

A voice behind Bert called out, "Honey, where's the hair dryer?"

Bert turned and shouted into the house, "Under the sink."

Annie Mae's eyebrows furrowed. "Do you have a new lady already? My goodness. Lucy just died!"

"Hold on." Bert disappeared into the house.

"That son of a gun. Do you believe him? I bet he killed Lucy so that he could be with the hair-dryer slut." Annie Mae jabbed her fist in the air.

"Maybe. Maybe not. We're here to find the truth ourselves." I glanced around the yard. Seeing Lucy's copious colorful flowers put a smile on my face. She'd had such a green thumb.

"No more Ms. Nice Guy. I'm going to make him come clean before we leave. With any means I have." Annie Mae stomped her foot on the ground. "Adulterous jerk."

"Right."

A moment later, Bert returned. "Okay, I've had enough of whatever it is you two are up to. You need to leave."

"First, the truth of your whereabouts the night Lucy died. Then we're gone," Annie Mae said.

"I don't have to answer you." He glanced over his shoulder.

"Fine. Then you'll have to talk to the police." Annie Mae pulled out her phone. "I'm sure they'll reopen the case once they find out your alibi was full of holes. Oh, and I am sure the

Savannah Morning News would love to hear about what we've unraveled so far. Adulterous husband who lied about where he was the night his wife died. Very suspicious. It'll get the tongues wagging. I think it'll be front-page news. And I bet we can get television coverage, too."

"Jeez. You are a pain in the ass." Bert narrowed his eyes. "I did not kill my wife."

"Then where were you? 'Cause you sure weren't fishing." Annie Mae stared at Bert.

Bert remained silent for a minute.

Annie Mae tapped her foot, her arms folded once again. "So? I played nice with you, and that didn't seem to work. Now I have to go and get all tough and mean on you. Would you like me to ask the question slower so that you can understand?"

"Not that it's any of your business, but I was with a lady friend at a hotel. Out of state. And I have receipts to prove that." Bert shook a finger at Annie Mae and me. "So back off."

I took a deep sigh. "You didn't kill Lucy?"

Bert shook his head. "No. I may be a cheater, but I'm not a killer."

"Well, goodie for you, taking your made-up moral high ground. Cheating okay, murder not." Annie Mae twisted her mouth.

I sucked in a breath. "Do you know anyone who would've wanted to kill her?"

He shrugged.

"Anyone who didn't like her or who she may have upset or got on their nerves?" Annie Mae asked.

"Lucy was sweet. But you, on the other hand, are irritating as hell." Bert waved a hand at Annie Mae.

"Funny, Bert." Annie Mae grinned. "I admit that I may be exasperating. But I was never a cheater."

"Hey." Bert teed his hands in a time-out sign.

"Sorry." Annie Mae looked down at her feet. "I was a little out of line. The sugar and all. I'm getting cranky, and you are pushing all of the wrong buttons with your coy BS."

Bert glared at Annie Mae.

Annie Mae glared back.

Soon they were in a staring contest, neither blinking or turning away.

I needed to figure out what to do next to get a lead. "We're going nowhere with this. But I wonder if you would let us borrow Lucy's cell phone."

"I don't think so." Bert put his hands on his hips.

Annie Mae broke her glare at Bert. "Please? With extra sugar on top?"

"Haven't you had enough sugar?" Bert half grinned.

"So, will you get it?" Annie Mae asked.

Bert stood there eyeing Annie Mae and then me.

Hoping to encourage him, I said, "It'll only take you a second to get it. You see, it's really important. Because…um…because…"

Annie Mae nudged me in the arm. "You see, Lucy took some pictures of Cat's kids and forgot to send them to her. And you know how much Cat loves her kids, and these are really special, one-of-a-kind pictures to her. So we desperately need the phone."

I added, "We promise to get her phone back to you."

"Please?" Annie Mae said.

"It's really critical," I added.

"*Fine* already. I've wasted enough time with you two. I'll do anything to get you off my back." Bert raised an eyebrow. "Stay right here, and I'll bring it to you. But then you must leave. Immediately."

A minute or so later, Bert opened the door and shoved the cell phone at Annie Mae. "When you return it, put it under that flower pot."

As we drove away, Annie Mae said, "I think that went well. Where to next?"

"How about you scroll through Lucy's call log and her texts? Look for anything that stands out."

While I drove, Annie Mae looked through Lucy's phone. "So far, nothing that says 'I will kill you' or anything like that."

"That'd be too easy, huh?"

"Besides calls to her husband and us, there were quite a few to the humane society and that antique store. Plus a few names I don't recognize. They could be her Bible study people."

"Since we're close, why don't we visit the grocery store next?" I suggested. "Maybe they can tell us if they noticed anything off about Lucy."

"This time you play bad cop, and I'll be good cop," Annie Mae said.

"How about we both just ask questions nicely?" I smiled.

"Bert's a jerk. He deserved my sugar-induced cranky attitude."

"Let's hope that we didn't anger him too much."

"Why?"

"I'm just saying that if he is still a suspect, that means he could be capable of violence."

"Shoot. Maybe I should have been nicer."

"Too late." My stomach twisted.

CHAPTER 8

*F*ifteen minutes later, we arrived at the Red and White Jones Food Market in Habersham Village.

A girl around eighteen years old stood at one of the three registers. Her red name badge read "Cynthia." The white linoleum floors had yellowed in spots that looked like permanent coffee stains. The place smelled of bleach and fresh-baked bread. Glancing around at the metal shelving and fluorescent lights, I thought it looked as though the store hadn't changed much since it'd opened in 1980.

"Good morning, Cynthia. My name is Catherine Thomson. This is Annie Mae Maple. We were wondering if your manager would have a few moments to talk to us."

"Are you Timmy and Teddy's mom?" Cynthia blushed.

"You know my sons?"

"Um, like, yeah, every girl knows them." She flipped her blond hair over her shoulder. "They're hot."

"Did you hear that? Your boys are hot." Annie Mae tapped me on the arm.

It unnerved me to hear my boys connected to that sexual term. "Can we talk to your manager, please?"

"Miss Susie Wells?"

"If that is your manager, then yes."

"Like, she left a while ago. I don't know if she's back yet."

Cynthia pressed a button on a speaker next to the register and spoke into it. "Miss Susie, you're wanted at register one."

A lady walked through the automatic doors, letting in a blast of hot air. The squeaky sound of a wheel on her cart echoed off the walls.

"While we're waiting for Miss Susie, I'd like to ask you some questions," I told the clerk.

"Yes, I'm single."

I raised an eyebrow, and my mouth fell open.

"Tell your sons. Either one, it doesn't matter." Cynthia popped a piece of gum in her mouth and chewed. "'Cause they're identical. Like, you know."

"Girls these days are not subtle, are they?" Annie Mae whispered in my ear.

"Cynthia, how long have you worked here?" I asked.

"Almost a year. But I only work part-time. Like, I still have school and all." Cynthia twisted her hair around her finger and popped a bubble in her gum.

"Do you know a customer named Lucy Valentine?" I asked her.

"She's a friend of ours." Annie Mae peered at a potted plant for sale at a table near the register. "I need a plant that is low maintenance. Do you have any that don't need a lot of water or sun or, well, anything?"

"I dunno. They should have a little white stick thing in the pot that tells you about them." Cynthia wiggled her hand.

Annie Mae walked over to the display and pulled out a white plastic stick. "Found it. 'Lots of sun, water every other day.' Way too much work for this one."

"Do you know Lucy Valentine?" I asked Cynthia.

"Didn't she…" Cynthia leaned in. "Slit her wrists?"

It made my heart sink into my stomach to think about Lucy being gone. "How well did you know her?"

"She came in here all the time. I'm, waaaaay younger than her. We weren't, like, friends or anything like that." Cynthia rolled her eyes.

"Can you tell me anything you may remember about the last time you saw her?" I asked.

"I have a picture memory. It's something like photosynthesis or something." She beamed as though telling me she had a genius IQ.

"Photographic?" I offered.

"Yeah. Right." She snapped her gum. "Like, I remember Lucy bought some peaches and some rolls. I also remember she was sort of weirded out. Like, she kept looking around every time my manager was in sight. Lucy's eyes kind of stalked her. You know what I mean?"

I said, "Not really."

Cynthia leaned in to me over the conveyor belt. "Like, it was kind of creepy."

A short, thin, redheaded lady wearing a tight, sleeveless pink dress offering ample cleavage approached us. "Did you need me?"

"Yeah. This lady here." Cynthia waved her hand toward me.

I stuck out my hand. "My name is Catherine Thomson, and over there is Annie Mae Maple." I pointed to the plant display a few feet away. One by one, Annie Mae took out the white plant stakes and read them.

Just then, Annie Mae called out, "I'm still looking for one that is low maintenance. Give me a few more minutes."

"Try the *dieffenbachia* or *pothos*," Susie called over to Annie Mae.

"Great. Thanks," Annie Mae called back.

I smelled a sweet fragrance near Susie. "Nice perfume."

"Oh, no. Just a new shampoo." Susie fluffed her hair. "You look familiar. You said your last name was Thomson?"

"Yes. My married name. I've lived here all my life, so you may know me by my maiden name, Argall."

"Your family owns the Sunshine Market on Forsyth, don't they?" Susie pursed her pink lips.

"Yes, they do."

"I'm really sorry about the burglary and your dad." Susie tilted her head and let out a small *tsk*.

"Thanks." My heart ached.

"After that happened, it scared a lot of businesses like us. We upped our security by adding new locks and alarms. I'm even thinking about getting a gun." Susie bent over and picked up some trash on the floor. "Cynthia, when you're not ringing up a customer, you need to clean up around you."

The whoosh of the automatic door sounded, and three children and their mom entered the store, followed by an elderly couple.

Cynthia popped another bubble and turned her back to ring up Annie Mae, who handed her a plant.

Susie had flawless porcelain skin. Her blue eyes were outlined perfectly in black liner. Given the slight wrinkles around her mouth and eyes, I put her age around late fifties, early sixties. I didn't see a wedding ring on her hand, or any rings, for that matter. She wore a stunning, gold Celtic cross necklace with a diamond that fell into her décolletage.

"Beautiful necklace," I said.

"From my boyfriend. It's from Levy's." Susie blushed while she touched her neck. "So, what can I do for you?"

"I'm sure you're busy. I just wanted to ask if you knew Lucy Valentine." I adjusted the purse on my shoulder.

Susie's face froze. Her eyes darted up to the ceiling and then back at me. "She was a regular customer here."

"Yes, I know. That's why we're here. We're trying to see how she was the last week of her life. If anything seemed different about her." I tried to make eye contact with Susie, but she seemed to be occupied with things around me.

She seemed familiar. Where had I seen her before?

Lucy's funeral.

"No. Nothing. She was fine." Susie gazed at her manicured fingers.

"Nothing unusual at all?" I asked.

Cynthia called out, "I need an over-ring." An elderly couple stood at her register.

"I have to go. By the way, we have peaches for sale if you need any. You'll love them, locally grown with no pesticides.

They'll melt in your mouth." Susie turned on her kitten-heeled sandals and walked away.

Annie Mae strode over to me, plant and receipt in hand. "I've adopted it. This thing can practically take care of itself. I wish I could find a man like this."

"Low maintenance?"

"Hell yeah. It'd be great if men had the little information stakes on them, too. I could've been warned when I married Ernie that he needed three home-cooked meals daily, frequent watering with beer, and lots of attention." Annie Mae grinned.

I laughed. "Andrew's would've said 'low maintenance, easy-going, needs lots of sex.'"

"Don't they all." Annie Mae and I walked outside to the parking lot. Steam rose from the blacktop.

Annie Mae opened the SUV's passenger door and put her plant on the seat. "Roll down the windows a crack. Do you think my plant will be okay in here?"

"You got a low-maintenance one. It should last forever. Plus, it's in the shade now." I pressed the button on the key and locked my SUV.

"Do you think I should have gotten two plants, so Marvin has a friend?" Annie Mae shrugged her shoulder.

"Who's Marvin?"

"My plant, Marvin Gaye. Now that it's mine, of course I needed to name it. I was thinking that or Jim Croce."

"Of course." I put the keys in my purse. "The antique store is only down the street. We can walk."

"So did you find out anything?"

"Yes. We've just met Bert's mistress."

CHAPTER 9

"The girl whose every other word was 'like'?" Annie Mae asked.

"No. The redheaded store manager, Susie."

"No kidding. The nice plant lady?" Annie Mae whipped her head in my direction as we ambled along the sidewalk in front of the small strip mall. "So that was the same woman who Bert fawned all over during Lucy's wake. Didn't she wear a black hat with a net hanging in front of her face?"

"Yes. It took me a few minutes to recognize her, too. And she wears pink lipstick. Could be the same color found on Lucy's note. Oh, and she smelled like mango shampoo."

"Call José. Have her arrested."

"Not so fast. I have no proof she killed Lucy. I just know that she's Bert's mistress. Lucy probably knew Susie was having an affair with Bert."

We made our way over to the Blue Belle Antique Shoppe a block away. The heat and humidity felt so thick you could cut it with a knife.

"You know, I feel like I'm losing weight doing all this sleuthing. Maybe I don't need to take water aerobics." Annie Mae huffed as she walked beside me. "With all the extra calories I'm burning up, I'm getting hungry."

I shielded my eyes from the noonday sun.

Annie Mae held her stomach. "I say after this, we call it a day and grab lunch at the Green Truck Neighborhood Pub. A big juicy burger with fries is calling my name."

"Let's go after we finish here." I grabbed the large silver door handle.

"Great."

"Ready?"

Bells attached to the tall glass door rang as we entered. We were greeted by a blast of cool air and the sweet aroma of potpourri.

"Smells like a florist." Annie Mae crinkled her nose.

A petite, sixty-something-year-old woman with short, teased brunette hair and wearing a lime-green-and-hot-pink dress with matching stilettos walked forward to greet us. "Welcome to Blue Belle. We are so glad to have y'all here."

She had a thick Southern drawl. Her perfectly made-up face was taut, her nose very small, her eyes slanted upward. She had a surprised look on her face because her eyebrows were raised even when her face was still. My guess was that she had undergone a full facelift with nose and eye job, lots of fillers, and regular Botox injections as well.

"Hi, I'm Catherine Thomson. My friends call me Cat." I shook her hand.

"I'm Scarlett Louise Montgomery." She pumped my hand. "You look familiar."

As we ended our handshake, I said, "My maiden name is Argall. You may know my family."

"Oh, yes." Scarlett let go of my hand.

"I'm Dr. Maple, but you can call me Annie Mae." Annie Mae stuck out her hand toward the lady.

"A doctor?" Scarlett said.

"PhD in fine arts," Annie Mae explained.

Scarlett opened her arms and turned slightly toward the center of the room. "Are y'all looking for anything in particular? We have a wide variety of antiques mixed with a tasteful assortment of new contemporary items as well. Very eclectic. Something for everyone, I assure you."

Picture frames, candles, knickknacks, and paintings were arranged on display tables. Some fringed pillows, along with throw blankets, were artistically displayed. Chairs, love seats, lamps, ottomans, and other household items adorned the space. A handful of crystal chandeliers hung from the cavernous twenty-foot wood-beamed ceilings. Jazz music played.

"You have a great store," I said.

"Why, thank you." Scarlett tipped her head. "Owning a business keeps me occupied. Mind you, there are only so many teas and luncheons that one can go to without being bored to death."

"I guess so." With four children and my family store, I had no idea what bored was. "Listen, when I have more time, I would love to look around."

Annie Mae picked up a candle, stuck her nose near the wick, then tipped it over to look at the price tag. "Whoa. A hundred bucks?"

I shot Annie Mae a look that I hoped conveyed "be good." "We're here to ask you some questions, if you don't mind."

"You're not trying to sell me something, are you?" Scarlett crossed her arms. "My door sign clearly states no solicitors."

"I have nothing to sell. Unless you want four kids?" I joked.

"Heavens, no." Scarlett's face softened to a smile. "I raised two boys, and now one is a father to a sweet little girl, Biddy. She's always giving me her artistic creations. She's such a peach."

"I bet she is." I nodded. "My girls love arts and crafts, too. They're now into making jewelry. I can't tell you how many times I've stepped on those little plastic beads."

"My granddaughter is making pottery now, some of it pretty good." Scarlett beamed with pride.

"Seriously, a hundred dollars?" Annie Mae held the candle and looked at Scarlett.

"It's imported, with the very highest quality wick and soy wax. And you'll notice it's in a crystal holder." Scarlett held her chin up. "Worth every penny."

"Not ten thousand of them," Annie Mae muttered.

"Do you have a few minutes to talk?" I asked Scarlett.

"About what?"

"One of your customers," I said. "We won't take up too much of your time."

"That should be okay. What do you need to know?" Scarlett asked.

The bells jangled, and a tall, medium-built man wearing a straw cowboy hat entered. He approached us.

"Pardon me, ladies." He took off his cowboy hat, showing thick white hair. Wrinkles accentuated his tanned skin. He touched Scarlett's arm. "Am I too early for our meeting?"

Scarlett looked at her silver-and-diamond wristwatch. "No, not at all. Excuse me, ladies. I just need a moment with this gentleman."

Annie Mae held onto the candle. "Is the wick made out of gold?"

Cowboy and Scarlett walked a few feet from us.

I overheard Scarlett say to Cowboy, "Can you come back today when we close? Around eight? I can give it to you then. We're packing it up so that it's safe for your journey." She kept glancing over at Annie Mae and me.

"I just can't believe you got it back. What luck," Cowboy said as Scarlett guided him farther from us.

Scarlett lowered her voice and stammered, "Yes. Lucky for you."

Then I couldn't hear them anymore.

"I mean, there should be a law against selling a candle for a hundred bucks." Annie Mae turned the candle in her hand.

"If I were you, I'd put it down. See the sign that says, 'You break it—it's yours'? You'd own the world's most expensive broken candle." I smirked.

Very slowly, Annie Mae set it on the display. Then she picked up a necklace and held it to my neck. "This would look great on you."

"Remember, I don't wear necklaces."

"That's right. Your strangulation phobia. You know, there is therapy for that." Annie Mae smiled.

My parents said I was born with the umbilical cord tightly

wrapped around my neck. Maybe that was why I had an aver-sion to all things to do with my neck.

The bell jangled as Cowboy left the shop. Soon, Scarlett was back at our side.

"We really don't want to be a bother, but can you talk with us now?" I asked Scarlett. "It's important."

Scarlett glanced from side to side. "You're in luck. It's not busy yet. I might be able to spare a few minutes. Plus, I'm parched. Why don't y'all come to the back, where I can fix us a glass of iced tea?"

We followed Scarlett through the maze of displays in the showroom to the back of the store. Scarlett pushed aside a thick tapestry curtain. We entered a hallway leading to an office.

Scarlett escorted us into a room with a huge mahogany desk, two overstuffed Victorian chairs, one leather chair, a coffee table, file cabinets, a refrigerator, and a small round table with a coffeepot and a potted plant. A floral rug covered the dark wood floor.

The scent of potpourri still permeated the air. There were several pictures on the wall. One showed Scarlett with an older gray-haired man, two tall boys, two women, and a young girl. I assumed it was a family picture.

Scarlett stood in front of the refrigerator. "I hope you don't mind, is sweet tea okay? Even though we have loads of out-of-town visitors, I just never got into the Yankee way of making unsweet tea."

Annie Mae and I both said yes.

She poured three glasses of tea and handed us each a glass.

"Thank you," I said. We sat across from each other. "I'm sure you've heard by now about Lucy Valentine."

Scarlett stopped midsip, and her neck reddened. "Oh, my. Yes. What horrible news. She was one of my best customers."

"That's what she told me," I added.

Scarlett placed her tea glass on a tile coaster on the coffee table. "She could spin a tale."

"You got that right. She was a hoot." Annie Mae sighed. "Still can't believe she's gone."

A raw, jagged pain hit deep in my stomach and twisted around. I missed Lucy. "Actually, that's why we're here." The tea drenched my taste buds in pure liquid sugar. I winced. "Do you remember the last time you saw her?"

Scarlett got up and walked to her desk. She flipped through a book. "A week ago."

The day Lucy died. "What do you remember about her visit here?" I asked.

"Why are you asking so many questions?" Scarlett shut the book and looked at her watch.

"Forgive me. Lucy was a dear friend of ours. We want to piece together everything that may've happened to her, to try to figure out why she…" My eyes watered up.

"Died." Annie Mae squeezed my hand.

"Why?" Scarlett's voice rose. "Didn't the police take care of that?"

"Yes, but we need closure," I explained.

"Hmm. I see." Scarlett shifted her stance.

"So what happened a week ago?" Annie Mae asked Scarlett.

Scarlett stood in the doorway, her back to us.

"Lucy mentioned a mystery box," I prompted.

"Oh, right. Sometimes we have orphan items that don't sell or have been around for a while. In order to make room for new merchandise, we gather them in a box and sell the whole lot, sight unseen, for one price." Scarlett looked down the hallway and then back at us.

"I love surprises." Annie Mae pointed to the potted plant on the coffee table. "Hey, I just got a plant like this. They're supposed to be easy to take care of. Are they?"

"Yes, very easy. I don't have time for finicky plants," Scarlett said.

"I hear you." A crooked grin lit up Annie Mae's face. "I'm going to name mine Marvin. This time I'll have a guy who's low maintenance."

Scarlett let out a giggle. "I never thought about naming a plant."

"Why don't we call yours Croce? After Jim, the singer. Your plant has that seventies vibe going on," Annie Mae claimed.

Scarlett nodded. "I guess so."

Needing to get back on track, I asked Scarlett, "Do you remember anything more about that box?"

Scarlett placed her palm to her forehead. She sat down. "My nephew, my new associate, assembled the items in the box Lucy got."

"Oh?" Annie Mae raised an eyebrow.

"I shouldn't have let him." Scarlett wrung her hands. "He's new, and I wanted to make sure there was a mixture of useful items and such. Since I didn't oversee things, let's just say that it didn't go as planned."

"What happened?" I asked.

"Nothing. Nothing." Scarlett's lips tightened. "He just didn't have the knowledge to know what went in the box and what shouldn't."

"Lucy told me she loved the plates, and especially a vase that was in the box." I took in a deep breath, trying to keep my emotions from overwhelming me when I thought of Lucy.

"That vase was hideous. No offense to your store and all, but you sold that here?" Annie Mae shook her head.

"Hideous?" Scarlett sucked in a breath. "I'm not sure what you mean."

Fearing Annie Mae might have insulted Scarlett, I quickly changed the subject. "What do you remember about the last time you saw her?"

Scarlett crossed and uncrossed her legs at her ankles. "Let me see. She came by the day of her accident. She said her sorority group planned a dinner that night at a friend's house." She shifted in her seat, as though sitting on pebbles. "That's really all I know. You may want to talk with that group of hers."

It struck me as odd that Scarlett referred to Lucy's death as an accident. But then again, maybe I was just oversensitive about Lucy. "Sorority group?"

"Her Bible study group at church only meets in the morning," Annie Mae said. "What group did she mean?"

"Let me think." Scarlett tapped a skinny finger against her cheek. "If my memory serves me, it had three Cs in the name, or it could have been a sorority like the Tri-Cs? I was a Delta Zeta at UGA."

I thought for a second. "It's not a sorority. It must be the Chubby Chicks Club. Our group."

"Why would any female purposefully call herself chubby?" Scarlett looked shocked. But then, she had that taut face with those permanently raised eyebrows and that stretched mouth, so who really knew?

"Um, do you see me? I'm a full-figured woman." Annie Mae adjusted her pastel blue blouse over her midsection.

"We aren't even all chicks." I grinned sheepishly.

Scarlett folded and unfolded her hands on her lap. "Lucy was a part of this chubby girls' club?"

"Absolutely. And we have one token male." Annie Mae slid her eyeglasses up with her index finger.

Scarlett's phone rang. With a wave of her hand, she excused herself and took the call.

Annie Mae and I stepped out of the office to give her some privacy.

In the hallway, packages wrapped in brown paper leaned against the wall. They all looked the size and thickness of framed paintings. One package was ripped in the corner, showing an ornate gold frame.

A row of boxes in a variety of sizes lined part of a wall. One box sat half-open, as if in the middle of being packed up, revealing the top of a blue-and-white porcelain item.

"She sure has a lot of stuff here, doesn't she?" Annie Mae pointed to another box that was open. "Hey, look here. One of those mystery boxes."

"How do you know?"

She pointed to a sticker on the side that read "Mystery Box."

"Good going, Watson." I patted her back.

"Why am I Watson? Why can't I be Sherlock?"

"Because you're a doctor, remember? Dr. Watson." I bent down and began to look through the opened mystery box.

Annie Mae followed suit. She pulled out a small, silver windup alarm clock. "I could really use this. I like old-fashioned clocks with their soothing ticktock. Like white noise to help me sleep. It's awfully quiet without Ernie around the house."

The curtain was pulled open, and a freckle-faced young man walked over to us. "Hi, I'm Zachary. Can I help you ladies?"

"We're just waiting for Scarlett to finish a call." I offered my hand. "My name is Cat, and this is my friend Annie Mae."

Zachary shook our hands.

"How much is this mystery box?" Annie Mae lifted the box.

"I'm not allowed to sell any of those. I sort of messed up the last box." Zachary ran his fingers through his curly brown hair. "I don't want to get fired."

"I wouldn't want that to happen to you, either. I just assumed it was for sale." Annie Mae set the box on the floor.

"Why don't you leave me your contact information so that I can call you when it's ready to be sold?" Zachary reached over and tore a corner of brown wrapping paper off a package nearby and then pulled a black pen from his pocket. He handed both to Annie Mae.

Annie Mae wrote down her information and gave it to Zachary.

Beyond the boxes, I saw a pile of recycling. "By the way, I see you have a big stack of newspapers back there."

"Those?" Zachary shot a thumb over his shoulder. "We use them for wrapping breakable items, which is pretty much everything in here."

"Where do you get them?" Annie Mae asked.

"Out of a recycling dumpster on Jones Street," Zachary told her. "About once a week, I head over there and grab a huge pile."

We needed to check out the recycling bins on Jones. Maybe we could find another newspaper similar to the one in Lucy's mystery box. Perhaps this could lead us to the killer.

"Does anyone here do the crossword puzzle?" I asked.

"I'm not much of a puzzle person. And I know Aunt Scarlett is hooked on that numbers puzzle." Zachary's forehead furrowed.

"Sudoku?" Annie Mae offered.

"That's it." Zachary bobbed his head up and down.

The office door opened, and Scarlett stuck her head out. "Zachary, you made it. Can you please go up front and open the register?"

"Yes, ma'am." Zachary waved good-bye to us and made his way to the front of the store.

"Pardon me, but I must get back to work." Scarlett guided us down the hallway. She pulled the curtain aside, and we walked through.

A jingle on the front door announced someone entering.

I shook Scarlett's hand. "Thank you so much for the tea and for your time. Would you mind if I called you if something came up?"

"Just in case we have some questions," Annie Mae added. "And I want to buy one of your mystery boxes. Zachary has my information."

Scarlett placed her business card in my hand. A large diamond sparkled on her right ring finger. "I'm so sorry about Lucy. I really am."

"Me too," I said. "Oh, and just one last question. Does anyone around here do crossword puzzles or write with a purple pen?"

Scarlett led us into the showroom. "I'm more of a Sudoku fan, and purple ink? I prefer red."

We said good-bye. Scarlett approached a group of four ladies who had just entered.

Annie Mae and I exited Blue Belle.

"Let's eat," Annie Mae said. "It's way past lunch."

As we drove to the Green Truck, I kept obsessing about the newspaper recycling bin on Jones Street and the crossword puzzle.

Did it mean that the murderer lived close by? Had he or she intended the crossword puzzle filled in with "your next" for someone else? Or had it reached the intended victim and then gotten disposed of afterwards in the bin?

One thing I knew for sure.

The killer was close.

CHAPTER 10

*W*e finished our late lunch and got back in my SUV. "Poor kid." Annie Mae buckled in.

"Who?" I put my key in the ignition, started the car, and blasted the air conditioner.

"That young man who works at Scarlett's shop. He seemed sweet but a little shaken up. Didn't he seem nervous about selling that mystery box?"

Parked in the lot, I became distracted while looking at a toddler who waited outside the restaurant with a group of people. He held a plush animal with one hand and a toy truck in the other. A woman held the little boy. I thought of my boys.

"Cat? Are you listening?" Annie Mae turned on the radio.

"Kids grow up too fast," I mumbled. When I thought of holding my kids' hands, my heart ached. Only the girls still let me hug and hold them. The boys, on occasion, would grant me a quick half hug. Hand-holding with them had ended years ago.

"Right." Annie Mae tapped my arm. "So what do you think about that kid in the antique store?"

I refocused my attention back on Annie Mae. "Zachary?"

"Yes, him."

"Sweet kid. Nervous but nice." I made my way out of the parking lot and onto Habersham Street. "Something isn't sitting right with me."

"The raw onions from your burger?"

"No, they were fine." I stopped at a red light at Victory Drive.

"Then what?"

"I think we need to go to the dumpster on Jones." I looked at my dash. My gas gauge was a hair from empty.

"I've always wanted to dumpster dive." Annie Mae put her hands together in a triangle. "I've heard people find expensive paintings and other treasures that are discarded. One thing, though: I won't eat food from a trash bin."

I grinned. "We need to be discriminating dumpster divers."

I turned into Parker's gas station and market. "I need to fill up."

"Since we're here, I'll get a diet soda with chewy ice. You want one?"

"No, thanks." I parked in front of a pump. "I'm going to call José."

"Then let me fill up while you do that."

"Thanks." I handed Annie Mae my credit card. She got out and started the pump. Then she left for the market.

I dialed José.

He answered on the first ring. "Are you in trouble?"

"Trouble? No."

"Good. I've been worried since you and Annie Mae have been playing amateur sleuths that you might've gotten yourselves in a bind."

"Not us." Not yet. "Anyway, let me get you up to speed. We've unearthed a few things that you should be aware of. I'm not sure what it all means. I don't know. Maybe it's enough to reopen Lucy's case."

"I'm not sure anything will. Tell me what you've got."

"First, Bert has a mistress. Her name is Susie Wells, and she's the manager at the Red and White."

"So? A lot of men cheat on their wives."

"Not mine." I couldn't imagine Andrew with another woman. I hoped he couldn't, either. Just to verify his loyalty to me, I needed to call him. "Oh, and Susie wears pink lipstick, like the color used on the note Lucy supposedly wrote."

José lowered his voice. "A lot of women wear pink lipstick."

"Yes, but Lucy wore red."

"Circumstantial."

"Maybe. But here's another biggie. Bert was not fishing in North Carolina with his buddies the day Lucy died."

"You have proof?"

"His friend James, who owns the lake house Bert was supposedly at, blinked two times."

José's voice rose. "So?"

"That meant that Bert was not with him."

I heard José snicker into the phone and then clear his throat. "Exactly what detective manual are you following?"

"I know it sounds bizarre, but James didn't want to rat out Bert. So we came up with signals he could use to tell us without really telling us."

"Blinking?"

"And foot tapping and sneezing. It got confusing. But in the end, he shook his head no when we asked him if Bert was with him fishing."

"You do know none of this will hold up in court."

"Fine. But Bert did admit to us that he was with his mistress at a hotel the night Lucy died."

"And where does this get you? People cheat and lie all the time. Welcome to my world of investigation."

"But at least we're making progress. You have to admit that."

"You gals should stop whatever it is you're doing. I think it could become a huge disaster. Or worse."

"But we're onto things." The words spilled out. "I found out that that newspaper with the crossword puzzle filled in with purple ink was taken out of a dumpster on Jones Street. Can you see if anyone around there was killed recently? I mean, I'm so close to finding the killer. Really, I know it. Right now, Annie Mae and I are going over to Jones to poke around. This could be it."

"You're not giving up?"

"Nope."

A deep sigh. "I'll get back to you."

Annie Mae climbed in the car and handed me my credit card and receipt. She put her drink in the holder and then fastened her seat belt. "You talked with José, right?"

"Yes."

"I bet he's really impressed with our detective work, huh?"

"You could say that."

But I wouldn't.

CHAPTER 11

*O*e parked in front of a row of houses on Jones Street, near Clary's Café. Live oak trees lined the brick sidewalks. I could see the spires of St. John's Cathedral peering above the housetops. José had just said that a lot of men cheated on their wives. Even though I knew I had nothing to worry about with Andrew, I still needed to hear from him.

"I'm going to call Andrew."

"Go for it. I'll get out and walk around a bit. You know, do a little surveillance." Annie Mae exited.

I also missed my kids and wanted to check and make sure they were all right. Since their generation did not answer their phones, I texted Timmy and Teddy: *How are you? Checking in. Call or text me. Love you. Mom.*

After I sent the texts, I called Andrew's sister, Pricilla, who had the girls for the weekend. No answer. They were probably at the beach. I texted: *All okay there? Sunscreen on? Life vests? Remember, Nina does not like her food to touch, and Nancy's Dora the Explorer nightlight is in her bag. Thanks for having them. Please call me ASAP. Love, Cat.*

I pushed my speed dial number one.

Andrew answered. "You girls having fun?"

"We're about to dumpster dive."

Andrew chuckled. "I'm afraid to ask."

"I have a weird question. Men cheat on their wives. You're a man."

Andrew interrupted. "Last time I checked. Where did that come from?"

"José mentioned something a while ago about how everyone cheats on each other. It's been gnawing at me. I know we love each other and all that. But still, I have to ask just to verify. So, yes or no? Would you ever cheat or even think about it?"

"By the way, that was two questions."

"Okay, then. Give me two answers."

"I can barely handle you. What would I do with another woman? So no, I am not cheating on you, and no, I won't cheat on you." Andrew laughed.

"Bert was having an affair."

"What a scumbag."

"I know, right?" I took a deep breath. "So are the kids okay?"

"All is fine. I talked to my sister an hour ago. They were heading back to the beach for the rest of the afternoon. The boys are still at work. Your mom and I have everything under control. By the way, did your dad ever mention any accounting issues with the store?"

"Not that I know of. Why?"

"I'm having problems trying to make the books balance. I'm sure it's just a learning curve, and I'll make it work."

"If not, I can always take a look at the books."

"Well, don't worry about that now. Enjoy your diving."

"Love you."

"Love you, too. Be good."

I met up with Annie Mae.

Annie Mae pointed. "Are we going to the alley over there?"

"That's where Zachary said he found newspapers to wrap stuff at Scarlett's. The same place that the recent purple-filled crossword puzzle must've come from. There is a possibility that the person who uses purple ink is around here. Maybe we'll find a clue. It's worth a try."

We made our way over to a graveled alley that butted up to the back of carriage houses. Many of the Jones Street houses were four-story Italianate with brick or stucco over brick. They had courtyards separating them from smaller two-story carriage houses.

We neared a large garbage can against a carriage house. Vines climbed the side of the brick exterior of the house. The trash emitted odors of rotting food.

"Whoa. That stinks. There is no way I'm going through that." Annie Mae held her nose.

"We'd never get the smell out of our clothes. Let's start over here. Look in these recycling bins." I motioned at a brown container with a bright yellow lid sitting in the alley. I opened one and found various plastic bottles, newspapers, aluminum cans, and glass bottles. "Let's search each one."

"You get this one. I'll do that one." Annie Mae rummaged through a bin a few feet down from me. "No antiques in here."

"Remember, we're looking for a newspaper crossword puzzle with purple ink." I walked to another bin past Annie Mae.

"Wouldn't it be great to find a painting worth millions? Remember when a lady in Manhattan found an original painting by Rufino Tamayo in a dumpster?" Annie Mae pulled out a newspaper from a bin. "Just saying, it would really supplement my soon-to-be retirement income."

"And four future college tuitions."

"So I say after we finish looking through these recycle bins, let's go down there and dumpster dive." Annie Mae pointed to a large, green trash receptacle, next to a house under renovation. "I feel lucky."

I flipped through some newspapers. Sports section. News section. Advertisements. Then I found the crossword. Not filled in. I shoved the papers back in the brown container. I shut the lid and moved to the next bin. I wiped the perspiration from my forehead with the back of my hand. My shirt stuck to my back.

Annie Mae held up a diaper by the tips of her two fingers. "These are not recyclable."

Poking in a container, I spotted a stack of newspapers under a white plastic bag. I yanked out the bag. As I pulled it toward me, it broke, releasing a hot brown liquid down my shorts and leg. It smelled like cola.

I picked up the mess that had fallen on the ground and put it back in the bin. I flipped through the newspaper. A crossword puzzle was filled in with blue ink and pencil.

The sun shifted, shading the alley, offering a little respite from the intense heat. My khaki shorts were spotted with the dark brown liquid from the broken bag. I had haphazardly pulled my hair into a ponytail. With the humidity, I knew it was frizzy. Something told me I didn't want to see a mirror.

A while later, I reached the last brown recycle bin.

Annie Mae ran her eyes up and down me. "You look like hell."

"It's the digging-through-trash ensemble. It'll be all the rage soon. Just wait."

"More like the homeless look." Annie Mae smiled.

We pulled out bottles and cans.

A few people walking by glanced our way. A guy in the group called out, "There's the Old Savannah City Mission on Bull Street if you need something to eat."

"We're not destitute," Annie Mae shouted after them. "I'm a doctor, and she owns a store."

A lady in the group made little circles near her head with her finger.

"We're not crazy," Annie Mae shouted as they walked away.

"I do look kind of needy." I shrugged and waved my hands over my shorts and hair. "Let's go, okay? We didn't find anything useful here."

Annie Mae pointed to the large green dumpster. "We still have that construction bin over there to explore."

"Fine." Feeling defeated and tired, I took a deep, energizing breath.

We trudged to the end of the block near Clary's.

"How do we get in?" I tried to push up one of the metal lids. "We can't get in this way. The top is too heavy to open."

"I say we climb in this side door." Annie Mae pulled a crate next to the dumpster. "We can use this as a stepstool."

"Are you serious? Let's call it quits. I need a shower. Clean clothes. A hug from Andrew and my kids. Maybe it's time to give up."

"Hold on there. What are you saying?" Annie Mae's hand was on her hip.

"Just that José said that nothing we found would hold up in court anyway." I turned and slowly walked away. "Let's call it a day."

Maybe I was fooling myself thinking that I could solve two murders. My heart sagged with despair. I'd failed. And I had started with so much hope.

"Oh, no, you don't." Annie Mae caught up to me. "Indulge me, Cat. There could be a million dollars in there."

I turned toward Annie Mae. "Or another diaper."

"Please. For me?" Annie Mae took off her glasses and gave me her big, sad brown eyes. "One dive, and we're done."

Annie Mae had spent the whole morning investigating with me. The least I could do was participate in her adventure. "You first."

Annie Mae climbed on the crate, hitching her leg into the side opening, her navy capris pulling at the seams. "Thank goodness my pants have spandex, or I'd bust these open and show my unmentionables."

With a thud, Annie Mae was in.

I jammed my head in the opening. Annie Mae was sprawled on top of debris. It smelled of sawdust. "Are you okay?"

"I'm fine. Join the party." Annie Mae righted herself as she dusted wood chips off her.

A dog barked nearby. A siren blasted in the distance. I climbed up, grabbing on the side of the opening, and maneuvered my leg. I scraped my shin on something. Could've been rusty metal. I couldn't remember my last tetanus shot. I knew every vaccination my kids had. But my own? I hoped it'd been less than ten years ago.

Inside, I got my footing, barely able to stand without hitting my head on the top. Light from the side door provided scant visibility.

"Isn't this cool?" Annie Mae picked up piece of wood. "A treasure hunt."

I climbed over white porcelain, navigating the uneven floor of debris. "Is this a toilet?"

The dumpster held various household items, cardboard boxes, some trash, and a lot of wood.

"Look at this old light fixture. Think it's an antique? Maybe Scarlett will buy it from me." Annie Mae held a small brass chandelier. "I'm keeping it."

A loud crash echoed inside. It sounded like someone had thrown a large object at the metal wall. I heard voices. A Coke can barely missed me as it whooshed past.

"What was that?" Annie Mae asked.

"Someone threw a can in here."

"I hope they throw something valuable next."

I sniffed. "Do you smell anything?"

"Now that you mention it, I do. Sort of smells like a campfire, which makes me think of eating s'mores. I'm kind of craving something sweet right now. That diet soda didn't do it for me." Annie Mae stood next to me, chandelier in one hand.

"I don't want you to panic, but I think something is burning." My stomach lurched. "And our only exit is there." I pointed to the opening we had just climbed through. Flames licked up.

Panicking, I began to pound on the lid, hoping to push it up and get fresh air. My hand stung with each hit.

The lid didn't budge. At this rate, we would suffocate. My eyesight was blocked by rising smoke. Dizziness overcame me as I tried to focus.

Annie Mae coughed and held her shirt over her mouth. "This is the end of my dumpster diving."

"I just don't want it to be the end of our lives." Finding a sliver of light enabled me to see my phone. I dialed 911.

"911, how may I help you?"

Gagging on the smoke, my voice came out shaky. "Please send a fire truck immediately to the alley on Jones Street near Clary's. There are two of us trapped in a green dumpster. It's on fire. Please hurry."

CHAPTER 12

"So I hear a call on the scanner. There's a fire in a dumpster on Jones, and two people are stuck inside." José took off his sunglasses.

A fire truck, an ambulance, and three squad cars lined the alley on Jones. A dozen or so onlookers gathered nearby. The smell of burnt wood hung in the air.

"Weird, huh?" I grimaced as I stood next to Annie Mae near the ambulance. A half dozen police milled about.

The fire truck pulled away.

"What's even stranger is that, right away, not only did I know those two people were female, I also knew their names." José took a deep breath and then exhaled.

"You must be psychic." Annie Mae nudged me in the arm.

"No." José scratched his head. "I knew that two of my friends were getting in way over their heads. I'm not even going to ask why you were in there."

"Good idea." Annie Mae nodded.

José put his arms in the air.

"Do you know what caused the fire?" I asked José.

"They found a burning cigarette butt around the dumpster." José twisted his mouth. "Another could have been thrown in and set the wood chips on fire."

"See?" Annie Mae stood arms akimbo. "Smoking is hazardous. It almost killed us."

"Thankfully, it didn't." I looked down at my leg, where EMS had cleaned and bandaged the scrape.

"Did someone purposely set us on fire?" Annie Mae asked José.

"I hope not," I added.

José said, "I'm not trying to throw shade on you, but what a fool thing—"

Annie Mae interrupted. "Throw what on us?"

"I meant that I'm not trying to chastise you about what you all are doing." The radio attached to his shoulder buzzed. He waved at one of the officers. "Gotta go. I'm glad you're okay. Stay out of trouble."

I gave José a thumbs-up before he left.

"Cat, I'll be right back. I see a former associate over there. I'm going to say hi and tell her about all the excitement I've had." Annie Mae strode over to a gray-haired lady in the crowd.

I glanced down at my phone. I had several missed calls and texts. Andrew, my mom, Teddy, Timmy, my sister-in-law, and Bezu. Savannah was a small town. I knew everyone would find out about Annie Mae and me and the dumpster. One by one, I called them back, assuring them that I was okay while down-playing the whole incident so no one worried.

By the time I completed the last call, Annie Mae was back at my side holding a chandelier. "I don't want to forget this."

"At least you got something nice. This day wasn't a total disaster." My shoulders slumped.

"Cheer up. I had fun." Annie Mae patted my arm.

"I wanted to find a killer. And now we're empty-handed." I plodded down the sidewalk.

"Not me." Annie Mae walked alongside me. "We did find out that Bert's a lying adulterer."

"But where does that get us? No closer to anything."

As we turned the corner and approached my SUV, I noticed writing on the windshield.

"What's on your windshield?" Annie Mae jogged to my car.

Her large breasts bounced up and down, and the metal on the chandelier clanged as she took each step.

I ran to the front of my SUV. The words, written in pink lipstick, said, "Back off Bert."

Annie Mae leaned on my SUV, pointing at the message. "Holy smokes. Is that a threat?"

"I'm not sure. But if it is, then maybe the same person who wrote this also just tried to incinerate us in the dumpster." I locked eyes with Annie Mae.

"See? Today wasn't a total disaster. We must've stirred up a hornet's nest, and now the killer is after us."

"And how is that good?"

"It means we are closer to solving your dad's and Lucy's deaths."

"Or getting killed."

"Let's stay positive, okay?" Annie Mae shrugged.

"Right."

My head spun with the implications of someone being after us. My husband and mom couldn't know about this, or they'd never forgive me for putting myself in danger. For that matter, I wanted to run the other way, too.

I loved my kids and family and couldn't imagine what would happen to them if something happened to me. On the other hand, I felt just as strongly about continuing the investigation and getting the killer off the streets.

I was torn.

Continue or run away?

CHAPTER 13

*A*nnie Mae leaned on my SUV's hood. She took a finger and touched the bottom of the letter B. "It's written in lipstick."

"Pink lipstick." A bell went off in my head. "Could it be the same used on the note found next to Lucy's body?"

Clouds rolled in. A crack of thunder sounded. The humid air smelled earthy and sweet.

Annie Mae took out her phone and began to snap pictures of the windshield.

I fobbed my doors open. "What are you doing?"

"Taking pictures, just in case it rains." Annie Mae pointed up. "It's getting dark."

"Good idea. But I think it'll take more than rain to get that off."

"Should we call José?" Annie Mae opened the passenger door.

"I will." I got in the driver's side and hit speed dial nine.

José answered. "Are you stuck in another dumpster?"

"Ha. No." To Annie Mae, I said, "He wanted to know if we were stuck in another dumpster."

"Funny." Annie Mae buckled up.

Back on the phone, I got serious. "So, listen, José. Somebody vandalized my SUV."

"Oh?" José asked.

"Someone wrote 'Back off Bert' on my windshield."

"Back off, like a threat?"

"That's what I'm thinking."

"With what?" José asked.

"Pink lipstick."

"Lipstick? So you can wash it off, right? It's not permanent."

"No. But Annie Mae took pictures of it, too, just in case."

"Nothing else is wrong with your vehicle?"

"No. I'm sure the message referred to Lucy's husband."

"I guessed that, too," José said. "Do you need a police report?"

"Should I file one?"

"If you need it for an insurance claim."

"No. But I do want proof about the message written on my windshield. And for someone to take a sample of the lipstick. Just in case it proves useful later on."

"An officer will be there shortly. Sit tight." José clicked off.

Five minutes later, a squad car pulled up.

A skinny, fresh-faced officer walked over to us. "Hey, are you the dynamic duo that was in the burning dumpster?"

"We're celebrities." Annie Mae grinned from ear to ear.

TEN MINUTES LATER, THE OFFICER FINISHED THE REPORT, took the sample of the lipstick, and left.

I struggled to see in the window through the lettering. "What a mess."

"We have to get something to wash that off." Annie Mae rummaged in her purse. "My makeup remover pads may help. I may have some tissue, too."

"Look in the backseat. I have a box of baby wipes."

"You still carry them around? The girls have been out of diapers for years."

"Yes, but they still get sticky fingers, and there are always spills to clean."

After I used a box of baby wipes, my windshield was clean, and we were on our way.

"What do you think that message meant?" Annie Mae asked.

"I've been thinking about that. It was missing punctuation, so I'm not too sure. Did it mean to read 'Back off,' then a period, then 'Bert'? Meaning Bert signed the message? Or did it mean leave Bert alone, and someone else wrote it?"

"Like his mistress?" Annie Mae suggested.

"I think we need to visit Bert and Susie."

"Since they're a couple, maybe they'll be together, and we'll get two lovebirds with one stone."

"That would be nice."

I drove the few blocks over to Bert's house and parked in front.

"Let's play detective." Annie Mae unbuckled and got out.

As soon as I climbed out, it began to sprinkle. The air smelled of wet soil.

Annie Mae held her purse over her head. "I'm getting wet."

"Run between the raindrops." I always said that to the kids, too, when they complained about getting rained on.

We sped up our pace, and shortly, we were standing under the awning on Bert's porch.

Annie Mae jabbed the doorbell a few times.

The door opened. Bert, in shorts and pressed shirt, looked us up and down. "What the hell are you two doing here again?"

"We need to talk to you," I said.

"Jeez." Bert grimaced. "Cat, you look like hell."

"It's been a rough day." I ran a hand through my hair, only to get it stuck.

"What's that smell?" Bert's nose crinkled.

"Scent of a campfire, right?" Annie Mae added.

Bert nodded.

"It's us. Perfume of the burning dumpster," I explained.

Bert raised an eyebrow.

"Never mind." I sighed.

Bert asked, "So what do you want this time? You've got two seconds, because I have even less patience for you two than I did the first time you showed up."

"What's with the message on her windshield?" Annie Mae asked Bert while motioning toward me.

"What are you talking about?" Bert held the door halfway open.

"The message 'Back off Bert' written in lipstick," I said.

"I don't know anything about that." Bert raised an eyebrow. "How do you know it's about me?"

"You're the only Bert I know."

"That doesn't matter. I didn't write any message on your car. You need to leave now." Bert began to close the door.

"Whoa, hold on there. It was written in pink lipstick." Annie Mae grabbed on to the door.

"So?" Bert furrowed his eyebrows.

"Doesn't Susie wear that color?" I asked Bert.

Bert blushed and looked at the ground.

"Speechless, huh?" Annie Mae observed.

"Bert, this is not looking good for you or your girlfriend. Yes, we know about your mistress, Susie. First we almost get cooked in a dumpster, and now a threatening message is left on my vehicle."

"What does that have to do with me?" Bert turned his palms up.

"You lied about where you were when Lucy died. That is suspicious in and of itself," I said.

"Your mistress may've wanted her competition out of the way." Annie Mae shook a finger in Bert's face. "So she killed her. Or maybe you schemed together to kill her."

"That's enough. You both need to get the hell out of here. If you don't, I'm going to get a restraining order." Bert huffed as he nudged Annie Mae away from the door.

"Oh, hell no. You're not going to restrain—" Annie Mae lunged at Bert.

I grabbed her arm. "Fine, Bert. We'll leave. Just know that you and Susie are on our list of suspects."

"If I ever see either one of you here again, I promise I'll call the police." Bert slammed the door.

"That went well." Annie Mae brushed her hair with her hand. "I think I'm getting this detective stuff down."

"How so?"

"You see how I made him nervous? That's called backing him into a corner."

"So?"

"Now that he's scared, he's going to have to react. Maybe we'll catch him doing something that'll prove that he killed Lucy. We'll have to keep close tabs on him."

"Not too close, or he'll get us arrested."

"I've never been in jail before. I wonder what it's like." Annie Mae held her purse over her head as we both dashed to my SUV. "Although I did play Roxie in *Chicago*."

"Somehow I think real jail is different from that." I fobbed my doors open and got in.

"He wouldn't call the police." Annie Mae plopped into her seat.

"I wouldn't put it past him." I turned the key. "He's still a murder suspect, which means he could do worse to us."

"Like what?"

"Kill us."

CHAPTER 14

"We need to go visit Susie. I hope she's still at work. I think the Red and White is open from nine in the morning until nine in the evening. But I have no idea how long she works." I pulled away from the curb.

"One way to find out." Annie Mae scrolled through her phone. "I'm calling the store."

Annie Mae held the phone to the side of her head. "I got some bad peaches, rotted with worms. I need to speak to your manager, Susie.…No. No. Don't get her. I'll just stop in later. How late will she be there?…Uh-huh.…" Annie Mae held five fingers up. "Great. Thank you. Bye."

Annie Mae turned to me. "We have a half hour to get there."

"We're only a few minutes away."

"Now let me look up some questioning techniques." Annie Mae tapped her iPhone.

"I'm sorry I got you into all of this."

"You don't have to apologize. This is the most excitement I've had since the last time Ernie and I were amorous. The week before his heart attack." Annie Mae looked at her phone. "He was quite the skilled lover."

"Too much information." I smiled.

"I do miss him." Annie Mae looked up. "If it weren't for the Chubby Chicks, I'd be so lonely. Don't ever tell José that."

Keeping my left hand on the steering wheel, I reached over with my right hand and held hers.

Annie Mae's eyes watered up. "I'm so glad I have you as a friend."

"Me too."

Five minutes later, I pulled into the lot for the Red and White grocery store and parked alongside a red VW Beetle.

"I have to get myself together before we go in." Annie Mae grabbed a tissue and dabbed her eyes.

"Take your time." I shut off the engine.

Annie Mae blew her nose into a tissue. "So I web searched 'questions to ask a killer,' and I only came up with killer interview questions. Neither of us needs a job, so that won't work. But I remember seeing on a TV show that when the motive is found, it can lead to finding the killer."

"A motive to kill Lucy?" My gut twisted. "I cannot think of one single reason. None."

"Of course you can't think of one, because you're not a murderer." Annie Mae stuck a finger on her forehead. "We need to get into the head of a killer. This will help us find him and prevent any more deaths."

I wanted the person who had killed Lucy and my dad behind bars forever. Ever since I could remember, I'd had this intense drive to right wrongs. One of my grade school teachers had often told me that I had to understand life was not fair. But I couldn't accept that. "So you're saying to find the scum, we have to think like scum."

Annie Mae nodded. "Yes, now you're on the right track."

"Money usually is the root of crimes." Although when my dad had died, nothing had been stolen.

Annie Mae rubbed her fingers together. "Money is a big reason."

"Bert could've wanted the money from Lucy's life insurance policy, assuming she had one. They were upper middle class. Bert did pretty well as an accountant, and Lucy had quite a client list as a designer, so I'm thinking they probably had a policy."

"Or maybe he wanted the house to himself, so he could walk around in his underwear. Some men like doing that. My Ernie spent more time in his boxer shorts than real pants. I used to buy him all sorts of colorful patterns and prints just so that I'd have something nice to look at."

I giggled. "Okay, we'll add that to the mental list of motives."

Annie Mae bounced in her seat. "Here's another one. The mistress could've been jealous and wanted Lucy gone so that she could have Bert to herself. Although I can't fathom why. Maybe that's just me."

I furrowed my eyebrows in thought. "Can you think of anymore?"

"What about her neighbor? The fight about the tree."

"You're right." I stopped in my tracks. "But why would she kill my dad, too?"

Annie Mae's eyes went wide. Then she hung her head. "I'm so sorry. I forget we're looking for his killer, not just Lucy's."

"Maybe it wasn't the same person. Who could've had a motive to kill both Lucy and my dad? There's nothing that connects them. Not Bert, not Susie, not the neighbor."

"Now that you said that, you're right. It doesn't make sense that it'd be the same person after both of them. Sorry, babe." Annie Mae put her hand on my shoulder. "What do you want to do?"

I twisted the ring on my thumb as I thought of my dad. This whole time, I had thought we were after his killer, too, and now I realized that Lucy's could be a different person. "No matter how long I live, I won't give up trying to find the person who took my dad's life. But I think we should focus on Lucy's case first. We're getting close."

"Did you just say 'case'? That makes this sound so profession-al." Annie Mae waved her hands. "Almost like we are legitimate detectives."

The clock on my dashboard displayed 4:50. "We have ten minutes to get in there and talk to Susie before she leaves."

"Since I didn't find any useful things to ask a killer, we're going to have to improvise," Annie Mae said.

"That won't be a problem. With four kids, my whole life is done on the fly."

THE AUTOMATIC DOORS WHOOSHED OPEN, AND COOL AIR GREETED us as we entered the store. Loaves of bread in white paper bags sat on a table in front of the registers. A sign read, "Just baked." Next to it was a table of peaches.

"It smells like a bakery in here. I'm getting hungry." Annie Mae lifted a loaf of bread and stuck her nose next to it. "I have to get this."

Cynthia stood behind the register, playing with her phone. She looked up at us. "Hi, again."

"Hi, Cynthia," I said.

"Just giving you a heads-up. The bread is good. But, like, I wouldn't get the peaches if I were you. Someone just called and said they've got worms."

"Oh, really?" Annie Mae strode past the registers while looking around.

Cynthia rang up a customer as Annie Mae and I wandered down an aisle.

"Do you see Susie?" I asked.

"Follow me." Annie Mae walked down the cereal section as she pointed to the boxes on the shelf. "What ever happened to Quisp? I loved that cereal."

"Gone in the seventies, along with disco, pet rocks, and feathered hair."

"Too bad." Annie Mae rounded a corner, and I followed. "That was my favorite decade."

We entered the dairy section in the back of the store.

Susie was leaning against a glass freezer door, talking on a cell phone.

"There she is," I whispered. "What are we going to say?"

"Not sure yet."

"I don't want to disturb her. She may be on an important call."

Suzie let out a loud giggle as she talked into the phone.

"Something tells me it's a personal call, not business."

I paced back and forth. "Now, what?"

"Let me handle this." Annie Mae grinned.

I raised an eyebrow. "What are you going to do?"

"Watch and learn." Annie Mae walked in front of Susie, then collapsed to the floor. "OOOOOWWW."

My heart practically jumped out of my chest. I immediately dropped down on my knees next to Annie Mae. "Are you hurt?"

She winked at me. "Bait."

Susie ran over to Annie Mae. "Ma'am, are you okay?"

"Oh, my ankle. I think I may've twisted it when I tripped."

Susie's face flushed as she knelt beside Annie Mae. Her breasts strained against the seams of her tight dress. "I'll call an ambulance."

"No. No." Annie Mae slowly sat up. She held her ankle in one hand and rubbed it. "I'm sure that I can stand up just fine. It's feeling better already."

Susie's eyes scanned the area. "What did you trip on?"

"A wet spot...no, maybe a bump, but it could've been..." Annie Mae stopped midsentence, obviously trying to drum up an answer.

"Did you get that filthy from falling on my floor?" Susie narrowed her eyes. "Hey. Weren't you two in here earlier? Yes. I remember you. You bought a plant, and..." She pointed at me. "You asked a lot of questions."

"OOOOOOWWW." Annie Mae gave me a sideways glance. "I may never walk again."

"You just said you could stand up." Susie stood and crossed her arms. "Is this a scam? Because we have video cameras all over, and our insurance adjuster will know if this is fraud."

Annie Mae motioned for me to grab her arm. "Help me up."

I pulled her until she was upright. She waved her hand. "Let me try to walk on my own."

Annie Mae wobbled a little, dragging her left foot. "I can walk. It's a miracle."

Susie examined us, eyes slit. "You're Lucy's friends. Bert warned me about you two snooping around and bugging him."

Annie Mae put her hand on my shoulder. "Bert who?"

"Ladies, I think you should leave." Susie pointed to the entrance.

"I love your lipstick. What brand and color is it?" Annie Mae asked Susie as I held her arm and guided her down an aisle. She dragged her right leg.

"Wrong foot." I whispered to Annie Mae.

Annie Mae began limping on her left foot.

Susie followed us. "That's it. I'm calling the police."

"No need," Annie Mae called back to Susie. "I'm feeling great."

Annie Mae looked at me. "Let's scram."

With that, we both jogged out the door.

"I forgot to get some bread. It smelled so good," Annie Mae said as we climbed into the car.

We sat in the parking lot, both catching our breath.

"What now?" I asked.

"Hell if I know." Annie Mae flipped down the passenger visor and opened the mirror. "This detective stuff is putting color in my cheeks."

"You do have a healthy glow."

"And I didn't even put blush on today."

Cynthia appeared and unlocked the door on the red VW Beetle next to Annie Mae's door.

"I've got an idea. Roll down your window," I told Annie Mae. "Excuse me, Cynthia. Do you remember me? Teddy and Timmy's mom?"

A pop of gum, then a head turn toward us, and then a nod. "Yeah, right. You were, like, just in the store."

"Yes, we were." I smiled.

"You don't happen to have a loaf of bread on you, do you?" Annie Mae asked Cynthia.

I nudged her in the side. "Don't worry about that, Cynthia. I was just wondering if you could do me a favor. But it has to be our secret." I put a finger to my lips.

89

"You mean I can't know either?" Annie Mae's voice rose.

"*All* of our secret," I said.

"'Kay." Cynthia leaned through the open passenger-side front window. Her straight blond hair fell into the car. She smelled minty. "It smells weird in your car, like a lit grill."

"It's our clothes. We were kind of at a bonfire a while ago," I said.

"Cool. So, what do you need? I have, like, a half-hour break and need to grab some chow."

"Sure, I'll be quick." *Think. Think.* "We're getting a gift for your manager, Susie."

"We are?" Annie Mae asked.

I winked at Annie Mae.

"A surprise gift. We want to buy her favorite lipstick, but we don't know what color or brand it is." I shrugged while flitting my eyelids.

Annie Mae gaped at me, eyes wide, as she sat in the passenger seat between Cynthia in the open window and me in the driver's seat.

Cynthia snapped her fingers. "Yeah, if you, like, asked her, she'd get all suspicious."

"Exactly." I nodded.

"Wow. Like, that is a problem." Cynthia narrowed her eyes.

"I know." I turned my hands over and sighed.

"Bummer, right?" Annie Mae agreed. "What to do, what to do?"

"I have an idea. Do you want me to find out?" Cynthia asked.

"Sure. Only if you want to," I said.

"Like, of course, I wouldn't let her know what I'm, like, doing. You know, the surprise and all." Cynthia pulled a phone out of her tattered black leather backpack. "Give me your number, and I'll text you."

I gave Cynthia my cell number.

Annie Mae looked at me and then at Cynthia. "Like, wow."

CHAPTER 15

"*H*ow did you do that?" Annie Mae asked as I pulled out of the parking lot.

"Remember, I have two hot teenage boys, which means I have a lot of girls hanging around my house."

Annie Mae smiled.

"Like wallpaper, I hang around. I listen and learn. Some teen girls love drama, like secrets. She seemed the type."

"Bingo."

"Once we know which lipstick Susie uses, we'll get it matched with the sample on Lucy's letter and my car."

Turning on my directional, I merged into the right lane on Drayton. "We're one step closer to an answer."

"I pulled some tricks out of my sleeve, too. Did you like my acting?" Annie Mae pointed to her chest.

"Your fall?"

"In a method acting class, I learned how to do one without hurting myself."

"The Oscar goes to Annie Mae."

"I would've settled for a loaf of bread."

"What next?" I turned a corner at the light.

"We've talked to Bert." Annie Mae held a finger up. "Susie and Scarlett." She raised two more fingers. "Who does that leave to investigate?" She held three fingers up.

"Ina, Lucy's back-door neighbor."

"Ah, yes, the tree person. And the threatening note."

"Let's hope she can give information that leads to the killer."

"Or she could be the killer."

"Let's find out."

I RANG THE DOORBELL. ANNIE MAE AND I STOOD ON THE FRONT porch of Ina Nesmith's peach-colored, two-story stucco home, which backed up to Lucy's house. There was a huge tree visible beyond the rooftop.

The door opened. A shriveled lady who looked a hundred years old answered the door. She wore a pink crocheted sweater over a blue cotton dress. A pair of glasses hung on a multicolored beaded chain. Her thin white hair was piled on top of her head in a tiny bun. A hearing aid was visible. "Yes?"

"We're friends of Lucy, your back-door neighbor." I pointed in the direction of her backyard.

"Lucy died. And she didn't live here. You have the wrong house." Ina shook her head. A bobby pin fell from her bun.

"We know that. We need to talk about the tree issue," Annie Mae said.

"The what?" Ina said loudly.

"Tree issue." I spoke clearly and slowly.

"You need a tissue?" Ina's eyebrows creased as she pulled tissues from her sweater sleeve. She handed one to me and one to Annie Mae.

"No, thank you." Looking at me, Annie Mae rolled her eyes. Then she turned back to Ina. "You wrote a note to Lucy about a problem with a tree."

"Remember? Over the roots?"

"Rooster?" Ina leaned in. "I'm sorry, ladies, I have a difficult time hearing." She paused. "Do you smell smoke or is only me?"

"It's us." Annie Mae straightened her shirt.

"Were you at camp?" Ina asked.

"I wish. I love s'mores," Annie Mae said.

"Ina, that's not important." I had to think of a different strategy to get answers from her. I pulled out a piece of paper and wrote, "Tree problem with your neighbors, Bert and Lucy Valentine." I handed it to Ina.

She slipped her eyeglasses on. She read the note and nodded. "Yes. We have a tree that borders both our properties. They claim it is more on their side, but I don't think so. Anyway, they had a plumber who said the roots were breaking their pipes, and he needed to cut them. I told Bert and Lucy that I wouldn't let them do it because my gardener said that it'll kill the tree and make it fall over on my house. But their plumber went and did it anyway."

"She's right. I've heard that once the roots are damaged, it weakens the tree. It could cause it to die and then fall," Annie Mae added.

Ina nodded. "It was trouble, that's all I knew. They could not just go and do something that may affect me. It just wasn't right. And I told them so."

"Did you threaten them?" I asked, even though, looking at frail Ina, I found it hard to believe anyone would be afraid of her.

Ina leaned toward us, hand behind her left ear. "Say what?"

"Threaten," Annie Mae spoke loudly and articulated every letter.

Ina adjusted her hearing aid. "Oh, that's better now. Say what you said again."

I repeated the question.

"Yes. I was going to call the zoning department on them. You know they used Hardie board on their house? That is not allowed in the historic district. They should've never gotten away with that." Ina shook a bony finger in the air.

"So, you weren't going to harm her?" Annie Mae asked Ina.

"Armor?" Ina's face scrunched up.

"Harm her," Annie Mae said.

"Say, what?"

"Never mind. Thank you for your time." I began to walk away.

Ina called after us. "Oh, and I liked Lucy. I really did. She was a nice lady, but that snake of a husband used to have a lady friend over when she was not home. That is just not right. My hearing may be gone, but my eyesight is pretty good."

Annie Mae and I stopped in our tracks.

We turned around to face Ina.

"Were you home last week, the day Lucy died?" I asked.

Ina nodded. "Yes. And I think she had forgotten her key."

"Why do you think that?" Annie Mae said.

"My kitchen window looks into her backyard. Her kitchen is in the rear of her house like mine is." Ina trailed off. "A lot of houses around here are built that way. Nice and solid, too. Not like the new houses these days that look like they'll fall apart if the wind blows."

"And you saw Lucy the same night she died?" I offered, hoping to get Ina back on track.

"Oh, yes. She must have forgotten her key. I saw her climb in her kitchen window." Ina narrowed her eyes. "At least I think it was Lucy."

"You don't know for sure?" Annie Mae enunciated loud and clear.

"It was almost dusk. Not too dark, but still, for me, it was a little hard to see."

"You saw a female climbing in the window?" I asked. "Although you're not sure who?"

"It looked like Lucy, but then again, it could have been someone else. I never thought about that." Ina pulled her sweater tighter around her.

It could be one hundred degrees out, like it was today, and old ladies still wore sweaters. Like they had broken internal thermostats always set on cold. "Is there anything else you remember?" I asked.

"No. But a while later, there were police cars all around her house. Lots of commotion." Ina's glasses slipped down her nose.

The sound of a phone ringing came from inside the house.

"Your phone is ringing," I told her.

"I better get that," Ina said.

We said good-bye and left.

Annie Mae turned to me as we left Ina's house. "I think we can safely cross Ina off the suspect list."

"Agreed." I fobbed to unlock my SUV and climbed in the driver's seat.

"That lady is too fragile to smash a spider." Annie Mae sat down.

"What about Ina seeing someone climbing in Lucy's house the night she died?"

"Who was it?" Annie Mae buckled up.

"Bert?"

"No. He has a key."

"Right. And it couldn't have been Lucy. When she left to get the dinner rolls, I remember she had keys in her hand." I bit my bottom lip. "Then again, she could've gone in her backyard for some reason and accidentally locked herself out, so she had to climb through the window to get back in."

"Yes. But what if it wasn't her?" Annie Mae adjusted her shirt. "Then?"

"That leaves the killer."

I locked eyes with Annie Mae. "Susie."

"So Susie climbed through the window, to do what? Kill Lucy?" Annie Mae tapped her fingers on the door. "She'd have to know that Lucy was there. Remember, Lucy was not supposed to be home. She had planned to be with us all night. Until she decided to go back for the rolls."

I twisted the ring around my thumb. "I know. I'm trying to understand why Susie was there. Maybe Susie lost her lipstick during an earlier clandestine visit with Bert. And she wanted to go back and get it before Lucy found it. And that night, Lucy surprised Susie, and Susie panicked and killed her."

Annie Mae looked deep in thought as her brows furrowed. "Hmm, possible."

"Maybe Lucy had already found it." I ran through some scenarios as I clenched and unclenched my hands around the steering wheel.

"What are you getting at?"

"I'm just thinking out loud." I turned on the air, folded my arms on the steering wheel, and put my head down.

"Are you okay?" Annie Mae's hand touched my back.

"One minute, I feel like we're close, then the next, we seem a million miles away." I sat up. "I'm trying to figure out what would've happened if Lucy found Susie's lipstick."

"So, you think Lucy chose her husband's mistress's lipstick to write the fake suicide note with?"

"Oh, right. Not likely."

"Here's another thought. Susie killed Lucy, then wrote the note with her own pink lipstick, and—" Annie Mae stopped midsentence. "Now that I just heard that out loud, it sure doesn't sound like a smart move at all."

I shook my head. "No. It doesn't."

"Susie seemed pretty smart. After all, even with my great acting, she figured out that I didn't really trip." Annie Mae turned her hands over.

I rubbed my temples. "We can't rule out Susie just yet. Let's think about this. She could've panicked after she killed Lucy and written the note with her own lipstick by mistake."

"Yeah. Maybe Lucy had it in her purse after finding it. Maybe later, Lucy wanted to confront Bert about it. But she was killed before she had a chance to. And Susie just grabbed the lipstick from Lucy's purse, not realizing it was her very own."

"Maybe," I said. "How does Bert fit into this?"

My head spun. I felt like we were going in circles.

Annie Mae held a finger up. "On the other hand, maybe he was there. And helped Susie kill her."

"Or he did it himself."

"I wouldn't put it past that jerk. Like I've said before, if a wife dies unexpectedly, it's usually the husband who did it." Annie Mae clicked her seat belt on. "Where to?"

Suddenly I felt that I had to call Andrew and ask if he'd ever kill me. It was like a medical student who studies symptoms and diseases and then he thinks he has each one. All this detective work had started to make me think that I could get murdered next.

"Give me a second. I'm calling Andrew." I dialed one on my phone.

Annie Mae nodded.

Andrew picked up. "Hey, hon, are you okay?"

"Do you think Bert could've killed Lucy? Or for that matter, that any husband could kill his wife?" I blurted out.

"Hello to you, too." Andrew laughed.

"So?"

A long sigh. "You're killing me."

"That's not an answer."

"I love you with all my heart. There's your answer. I would never harm you. I can't speak for other husbands and how they feel about their wives."

"Love you, too." I ended the call.

"So?" Annie Mae asked.

I shook my hand. "This whole sleuth thing is making me paranoid. I feel like I'm losing my mind."

"Then let's stop."

"Maybe we should. Where has this gotten us so far? Almost burnt like marshmallows. Chased out of a grocery store. Oh, and Bert threatened to put a restraining order on us."

"Stellar day, huh?"

"Stellar?"

"We did get a lot of attention from the dumpster thing." Annie Mae looked in the passenger visor's mirror. She patted her hair. "I kind of liked the celebrity status."

"I could do without it."

"You know, I think we're really a great team. Too bad Bezu is missing out."

"Maybe she's better off."

My phone sounded with a text. "Looks like Cynthia came through."

"What does it say?"

I read it out loud to Annie Mae. "Revlon. Super Lustrous. Fuchsia Shock."

CHAPTER 16

*W*e went to the local Walgreens, bought the lipstick, and then we called José. He told us to meet him in the parking lot near the Forsyth Park tennis courts.

Annie Mae and I got there just after six in the evening. José pulled up in a white Explorer with the Police Department logo on the side.

Annie Mae and I got out of my SUV and greeted José.

I handed him the lipstick.

"First, I'm surprised to still see you in your dumpster diving outfits." José twisted the stick up. "Second, this is not my color."

"Funny, José." Annie Mae eyed him. "Although, with your olive skin tone, I can see you in more of a maroon or red."

José cleared his throat. "Cat, you asked me to look into recent deaths of anyone who lived near Jones Street."

"And?" I asked, my heart accelerating in anticipation.

José looked down at his phone. "There was a hit-and-run that killed a gentleman who lived on Jones. The accident happened the same day as the date on the newspaper Lucy found."

I wondered if that was the person for whom the second crossword puzzle had been meant.

"Holy smokes." Annie Mae's mouth hung open.

"Who was he?" My voice rose.

José glanced at me, then at Annie Mae. He looked down at his cell. "Michael Esker, age sixty-three, owned Quickie Loan & Pawn. He was a Grand Knight at the Knights of Columbus. He suffered a fatality after a hit-and-run on the corner of Clary's while he headed to his Wednesday morning Bible study. One eyewitness saw an older-model green sedan, a Lincoln or Buick, driving away from the scene. But that's our only lead."

"Poor guy." Annie Mae sighed.

"That name sounds familiar." I ran through people my dad's age in my mind. "Esker. Esker. I think I knew him, but I can't remember from where."

José held up the lipstick. "I'll get this analyzed against the lipstick on Lucy's note and the message from your windshield."

"I really appreciate it." I gave José a hug, but because of his height, I hugged his waist with my head on his chest. "I don't want you to get fired over it."

José patted my back. He smelled sweet and spicy. "No problem. I have a buddy in the forensics laboratory who owes me a favor. Trust me, he'll do it without anyone finding out."

With a wave, José climbed in his Explorer and drove out of the parking lot.

Rounding the corner by the tennis courts, Mr. Phong had headphones on and sang out loudly as he strode on the path. "All da move like da Jagger. I got the mooove like a Jagger." He nearly bumped into Annie Mae and me.

I stepped out of the way and made eye contact with Mr. Phong. I smiled and waved. He grinned from ear to ear and waved back. I noticed a ruby-stoned ring on his finger as he flapped his hand and nodded. He continued walking and singing.

"That is one strange cat," Annie Mae said. "But he sure seems like a happy guy."

Annie Mae and I got in my SUV. It was after six in the evening. "I wonder if my mom knew Michael Esker."

"The Grand Poobah?"

"He was a Grand Knight, not a Flintstone." I grinned.

"I'm going across the street to the Sentient Bean and grab a scone. You want anything?" Annie Mae started to get out.

"No, thanks." I hoped I wouldn't lose my dear friend to a heart attack the way she'd lost her husband, who'd had the same junk food addiction. We'd had this conversation, and she always said that she knew how to eat right and that one day she would.

I started the engine and put the air on. My phone rang. The caller ID said "Mom." I picked up.

Yunni said, "What you doing? All my friends call me to tell me about you and the fire. You okay?"

The Sunshine Market closed at six. I knew her routine. She was cooking dinner and watching the news. "I'm fine. I was just thinking of calling you. You're at home, right?"

"Yes. Why you ask?"

"I'm at Forsyth Park."

"You are close. Come to my house. I fix dinner for you. Making your favorite, bulgogi. Is Annie Mae with you?"

"Yes."

"She come, too. Lots of food."

"No, thanks, not tonight."

"Okay, fine, you miss out. Tadcu come here for dinner. Your boys, too. Maybe none left after. So no problem."

"Another time, okay?"

"Sure."

"Listen, do you remember a Michael Esker?"

"I read in newspaper. He died."

"Yes, I just found out."

"I talked to some friends. Found out he hit by car. Very sad," Yunni said.

"I know. But did you know him?" I asked.

"Yes. Your father business partner," Yunni said.

"Business partner?" I repeated, my voice rising. "For Sunshine Market?"

"Different business before store. Didn't work out."

I felt blindsided. I had no idea there'd been another enterprise before Sunshine Market. My parents never failed to surprise me. There was a good chance my kids would find out things about me after I died that they had never known before, even though I felt like an open book. "What kind of business?"

"Cars. Rebuilding, trading. Buying, selling. Complicated. Lots of time at junkyards and auctions. Dirty."

"So Dad and Michael worked together?"

"And three more men."

"Who were they?"

"Let me think." Yunni took a deep breath. "Davy O'Brien, Micky Zwick, and Peter Matthews."

"What happened to the business?"

"Your dad not talk too much about what happened. But he got out. They all did. No matter. After all that, your dad made money from some investment, and we started our store. Oh, honey, my food going to burn."

I tried to wrap my head around why both my dad and another former business associate were now dead within two months of each other. Was there a connection or just coincidence? Was the crossword puzzle somehow related to both deaths? I needed to talk to O'Brien, Zwick, and Matthews. "Okay, Mom, thanks. Love you."

"You, too. Plenty of food if you change mind." She clicked off.

My phone buzzed. Low battery. I plugged it into the car charger.

Annie Mae opened the passenger door. She had a scone in one hand and a drink in the other. She handed me her drink. "Can you grab this?"

I put the drink in the holder as Annie Mae sat down. "My mom just called."

"How is she?"

"Good. She invited us to dinner."

Annie Mae held up the scone. "Too late."

"I told her next time." I stared out the window, my eyes transfixed on a spot on my windshield. "My phone is almost dead. Can you look up a Davy O'Brien, Micky Zwick, and Peter Matthews for me, please?"

"Who are they?" Annie Mae tapped her phone.

I went over my conversation with my mom while turning my dad's wedding band on my thumb.

A few minutes later, Annie Mae looked over at me. "Cat. Davy O'Brien is dead."

My stomach took a free fall. "Can you find out what happened?"

A few minutes later, Annie Mae said, "He died last month. It looks like an accident. He fell from a building on Bay Street. Freaky, huh?"

A chill ran over my entire body. Even my hair felt like it stood on end. I could barely speak. Was someone killing off all of the partners in my dad's car business? "What about Zwick and Matthews?"

Annie Mae tapped her iPhone. She turned toward me. "Can't find anything on Peter Matthews. But it looks like Micky Zwick is still in Savannah and, as far as I can ascertain, still alive."

"How do you know he's still alive?"

"No obituary on him." Annie Mae continued to tap her phone. "Still can't find anything on Matthews, just Zwick."

I felt a wave of calm wash over me. "Can you find an address for Zwick?"

A moment later, Annie Mae looked up. "Forty-nine Barnard Street. We can walk from here."

I shut off the car. "Let's go."

CHAPTER 17

"At this pace, I'll burn off that scone," Annie Mae huffed. "But you need to slow down. I can't keep up with you."

My natural stride tended to be pretty brisk. Andrew and the kids were always telling me to slow down. I came to a halt when I realized I was speed walking. "Sorry."

"What's the rush?" Annie Mae stopped, leaning over and panting. "Is something on fire?"

I paused. "Just glad it's not us."

"I hear you." Annie Mae stood straight. "Okay, then, dial your pace back a few notches. We'll get there just the same."

We waited at the corner of Park to cross over Whitaker.

Cars whooshed by while birds chirped in the tree above us. On the playground, the sounds of kids' laughter filled the air. A few joggers went by. The scent of freshly cut grass filled the air.

A green car coming toward us seemed to speed up as it neared. Just before it reached us, it ran up on the curb where we stood. Instinctively, I grabbed Annie Mae and yanked her back. She lost her balance, falling into an azalea bush with me half on top of her as the car swerved back onto the street.

Finding my footing, I dislodged leaves from my shirt as I wedged my way to a standing position. I held my hand out. Annie Mae grabbed it and pulled herself up. She had some twigs in her hair. Her pants hung below her waist.

Annie Mae grabbed my arm, her eyes open wide. "I think you just saved my life."

"Are you okay?" I asked.

"Thanks to you, I'm not roadkill." She let go of my arm and pulled up her pants.

I raced to the corner and looked down the street, hoping to catch the make and the model of the car or the license plate. I walked back to Annie Mae. "They're gone."

"Cat, you don't think that car meant to hit us, do you?"

"I don't know. José said that a green sedan killed Michael Esker. And it was a green car that just jumped the curb and almost got us. Coincidence or not?" My stomach churned as though bubbling acid was percolating in it.

Annie Mae brushed her shirt. Azalea leaves fell from her. "I guess it wouldn't surprise me with all that has happened today."

"Me either."

Annie Mae pulled her shoulders back. "It's been an exciting day, hasn't it?"

My legs felt restless, as though I needed to run. And keep on running as though someone were chasing me. But who was it?

CHAPTER 18

"*S*hould we call José about us almost getting run over?" Annie Mae strode alongside me as we crossed Whitaker Street.

"I hate jumping to conclusions." Although I did feel like we were onto finding the killer. I scanned the area, looking for any wayward vehicles. I didn't want Annie Mae to worry; I was fretting enough for both of us and then some. "That could've been a student driver. When Timmy and Teddy learned to drive, they spent more time curb hugging than staying on the street. I'm just saying."

We walked down Park Street and then took a right on Barnard. Before long, we stood in front of a three-story brick colonial home.

"Whoa. It's gorgeous." Annie Mae climbed the red brick stairs.

"My dad looked at one like this a long time ago."

"Did he want to move?" Annie Mae pushed the doorbell.

"No. He wanted to get some investment property and rent it out to college students, as extra income."

I heard a click, then the rattle of a chain hitting against wood. The door opened to a lady of average height and build with short brown hair. She wore light green scrubs. "Good evening."

"Hi. I'm Catherine Thomson, and this is Annie Mae Maple. Please excuse our appearance. We haven't had a chance to change yet. I'm sorry we look so unkempt."

"I'm Karen." She shook our hands. "No need for apologies."

"Are you a relative of Mr. Zwick?" Annie Mae asked.

"No. Although I've been working for the family for years, so I feel like a relative. So, what can I do for you ladies?"

"A long time ago, my father was a business partner with Micky Zwick."

"Oh?" Karen squinted as she looked at us. "So you're friends of his?"

"Sort of," Annie Mae answered.

"It's a long story." I glanced around, trying to find the words to express what I wanted to say. "If at all possible, I would like to talk to him."

Karen shook her head. "That's impossible."

"He's dead?" Annie Mae asked.

My heart skipped.

"Oh, no. No. He just took his medication. It knocks him out." Karen brushed a hair from her eyes.

"Is he ill?" Annie Mae asked.

"He has been suffering from amyotrophic lateral sclerosis. The only thing we can do is ease his pain." Karen guided us into the foyer.

"Lou Gehrig's disease," Annie Mae whispered to me as we entered the house.

I asked Annie Mae, "How did you know that?"

"In the play *Thirty-Three Variations*, the main character, Dr. Katherine Brandt, suffers from it."

The house smelled of rubbing alcohol and wood cleaner. We stood in a foyer.

Karen closed the door behind us. "May I offer you anything to drink?"

Annie Mae shook her head.

"No, thanks," I said. "I'm so sorry about Mr. Zwick."

"He has a few more years left, at this rate. He's in good spirits and seems to have accepted his condition." Karen led us into a sitting room.

"Can I leave my name and number for him? He can call me when he gets up." I dug in my purse.

"We have urgent business to speak of with him. We're investigating," Annie Mae said.

"Are you working with the police department?"

"No," Annie Mae mumbled. "But we are good friends with someone in the department. Not that that is either here or there."

"Let me get you my information." I took a pen and tore the address part of my deposit slip from the back of my checkbook. I wrote my cell number and my maiden name on the back, along with my dad's name. "Please have him call me when he can."

"I'm not sure when that will be." Karen took the paper from me and tucked it into her shirt pocket.

"It doesn't matter when. Whenever he can call, it'll be fine. Thank you."

Annie Mae put her hands up. "We can let ourselves out. Thanks for your time."

We walked outside and down the front steps onto the sidewalk.

Annie Mae trailed after me. "Thank goodness he's still alive, huh?"

"Yes."

"Unlike the other partners."

"I know. Why did my dad and two of his other business partners all die in the past two months?"

"Although I'm only playing a detective, I can tell you that it's beginning to feel like someone has it out for that business group your dad was once involved in. Not that I want you to worry or anything. But then again, Micky is still alive, and as far as we know, so is Peter."

"Yes. At least for now."

"It could be all one big coincidence, right?"

"Or like you just said, someone has it out for all of them." A pain ran between my eyes. I could feel a strong headache coming on. "If that's true, then who is he or she, and is he or she killing them?"

"And since we seem to be onto the killer, will we be next?"

CHAPTER 19

"*H*ere's the thing. Until I hear back from Micky, it's all speculation." We sat in my SUV with the air running. "The only thing we know for sure is that they all knew each other and were once business partners. All of their deaths were different."

"If the deaths were similar, then it would link them to one killer," Annie Mae agreed. "I guess you're right. It's only conjecture now. What do you want to do next? Since we have no idea when you'll hear from Micky."

"I don't know." I tapped my dashboard with my finger. "It seems unlikely that their deaths and Lucy's death are connected. She had nothing to do with their business. Someone different killed her."

My phone rang. After looking at the caller ID, I answered, "Hey, José. I'm putting you on speaker so Annie Mae can hear, too."

"You gals staying out of trouble?" José asked.

"Of course we are staying out of trouble." I rolled my eyes at Annie Mae.

But her response was, "We almost got hit by a car."

"Did I hear Annie Mae say that a vehicle almost hit you?" José's voice rose.

Annie Mae smiled. "Don't worry. Cat saved me with her

maternal instincts. She grabbed me and pulled me from getting hit just as the car ran up onto the curb directly at me."

"I'm sure it was a student driver. Kids, huh?" I raised an eyebrow at Annie Mae.

"What about all the business partners getting killed?" Annie Mae said into the phone.

"What?" José asked.

I told José what I knew about my dad's defunct business and the men involved. "However, there are no leads to who may be killing them off. And I wasn't able to talk to Micky and don't know where Peter is."

"Maybe Peter is the killer of Cat's dad and the other business partners," Annie Mae offered. "He's not going to bother with Micky because of his condition."

"I'm not sure what you have amounts to anything," José said. "Might be happenstance."

"But there may be something there. You have to admit that." Annie Mae nodded at me.

"Maybe," I replied.

José sighed. "Listen, forensics gave me the results of the lipstick analysis."

"Now we're getting somewhere," Annie Mae said.

José continued. "Looks like the lipstick you gave me is a color match with Lucy's note and with the message left on your window."

Annie Mae held her palm up and high-fived mine.

"I knew it." My heart lightened. We were finally making progress. "What do we do now?"

"Arrest her, that's what you do. Right, José?" Annie Mae shook her finger at the phone. "You throw her sorry little butt in the slammer."

"No. That's not how it works," José said. "I'm in the area now. I'll see if Susie will be cooperative if I stop over and ask her some questions."

"Can we go with?" I asked.

"I don't think she wants to see us after what happened at the store," Annie Mae warned.

José's voice lowered. "I'm afraid to ask. What happened at what store?"

"I used some acting skills and fell to the ground in Susie's store to get her attention," Anne Mae admitted. "And then she found out that I really didn't fall. Do you believe she actually accused me of pulling a scam? Of course, we weren't conning her, just investigating. Long story short, we sort of had to run out of the store since she wanted to call the police."

José took a deep breath. "Let me handle talking to Susie. Whatever it is you all are doing is half-assed, and I'm surprised you haven't gotten into more trouble."

I winced. "Actually, Bert's going to put a restraining order on us if we don't leave him alone."

"Yeah, do you believe that jerk?" Annie Mae said.

I shook my head at her.

"Can't you just arrest Susie?" she addressed the phone. "Why do you have to talk to her? She killed Lucy. You have proof now."

"We only have proof that there is a match with the lipstick and the messages. Not that it was her lipstick," José pointed out.

"So, what do you want us to do?" I asked José.

"Stop. Go home. Let professionals handle this."

Annie Mae said, "But José, had it not been for Cat and me doing all that we did, you wouldn't know what you know now."

"Yes. I have to admit, even as haphazardly as you two have been going about whatever detective work you've done, you did find a connection. But it has yet to be seen if that connection amounts to solving a crime."

"But it just may," I said.

"Do you think we'll get a medal of honor or anything?" Annie Mae asked. "That'll look great next to all the acting awards I have."

José chuckled.

Annie Mae hutted. "I think you should deputize us."

A fire truck zoomed by, muffling José's answer.

Annie Mae raised an eyebrow as she pointed to the phone.

Then we heard José say, "Gotta go, ladies."

He clicked off.

"I think he said yes?" Annie Mae said. "He deputized us, right?"

I shrugged.

"Let's just assume that he did."

"What do we do now?" I asked Annie Mae as I pulled out of the parking lot. "Maybe José is right about it all meaning nothing. Should we just give up?"

"This is not over until the fat lady sings, and I haven't sung a note yet. I say we question Susie. We're hot on her trail. We need to strike while the iron is hot."

"How many more clichés can you fit in one sentence?" I laughed.

"Let's make like a tree and leave. To Susie's."

CHAPTER 20

nocking on Susie's door, I ran through questions I could ask her. Only one question needed answering. Had she killed Lucy?

Annie Mae banged on the door again. "Does it smell like onions out here?"

I looked around and recognized a plant. "I think you smell those—Chinese chives."

"This whole situation stinks, if you ask me," Annie Mae said. "Adultery, murder."

The door opened. Susie wore the same pink dress she'd had on earlier. A cell phone was in one of her hands. "Not you two. I'm going to call the police."

"You don't have to. We've been deputized. So we *are* the police." Annie Mae pointed to her chest.

I caught my breath. Had Annie Mae really just said that? I smiled weakly as Susie looked at me.

"And we're here to find out if you killed Lucy." Annie Mae moved toward the door.

Susie stood in the entranceway, neither coming onto the stoop nor retreating inside. "You two are freaking nuts. The police need to take you away. I'm calling them now."

Before she made the call, I had to know. "Where were you when Lucy was killed?"

"None of your damned business." Susie folded her arms and jutted her jaw.

"Oh, but it is our business now that we are representatives of the Savannah Police Department." Annie Mae nodded.

Susie raised an eyebrow. "I'm still not buying that. Matter of fact, I'm calling the police just to confirm it."

"Oh, no. You don't have to do that." Annie Mae waved her hand.

I stepped backward. "Really. Don't bother."

Susie dialed and then spoke into the phone. "I have two women at my house impersonating police officers."

I began to saunter away, Annie Mae right behind me.

A moment later, a white Ford Explorer, lights flashing and siren blaring, came to a halt in front of Susie's house.

I froze in my tracks and held my breath. "That was quick."

Annie Mae grabbed my hand. "Uh-oh."

The siren stopped. Climbing out of the Explorer was José. His eyes were narrowed as he marched over to Annie Mae and me. "What in the hell are you two doing? You've committed a serious felony."

"Didn't you deputize us?" Annie Mae asked.

"I did no such thing." José put his hands on his hips. "You're lucky I was on my way over here anyway. Any other officer would not be so kind. Jeez. Now I have to figure out how to get you two out of this mess."

Susie's kitten heels clicked down the sidewalk and she stopped right next to José. "Are you here to arrest these two idiots?"

"Ma'am, I'm responding to your call." José smiled, showing his straight white teeth, which shone bright next to his olive skin.

"Oh my, you are so tall and handsome." Susie moved next to José. "And you smell so good, too."

"I'm Sergeant José Rodriguez." He stuck out his hand. "How may I assist you?"

Susie wrapped both of her hands around his. "My oh my. Even your hands are strong." Susie looked José up and down.

He cleared his throat. "Did you want me to take these two off your property?"

"Yes, get rid of them, but you can stay if you need to fill out a report or anything. I could get you something cool to drink." Susie pulled her shoulders back and fidgeted with her hair.

"No, thank you," José said.

"Anytime you happen to be in the neighborhood, you're welcome to stop by and check on me. I'm single, and it doesn't hurt to have police protection keeping an eye on me." Susie sighed.

"Hey! You're not single. You're with Bert," Annie Mae said.

"No. Not really. I mean, we're not serious." Susie blushed.

José stepped back, smiling. I knew that smirk. José had that cocky grin that meant he knew that he could get anything he wanted out of someone.

"So what do you want me to do about these two?" José leaned into Susie. "I'm sure they meant no harm."

Susie flipped her hair from her eyes. "Maybe. But they were pestering me. Asking me all sorts of questions. They think I murdered someone. Can you imagine?"

"Really? You? I can't conceive of such a thing." José put on a half grin. "I bet you did nothing wrong."

Annie Mae rolled her eyes at me. I think she knew what José was doing as well. I was going to keep quiet and see if he got what he wanted.

Susie smoothed her dress. "I didn't. I was with someone at a hotel in North Carolina when Lucy died. So it would've been impossible."

"I believe you." José looked over at me and Annie Mae and then at Susie. "And I'm sure you have proof as well."

"Of course I do. Plus, I won a karaoke contest that same night. They gave me a dated certificate and everything. Not that I have to answer to those two." Susie pouted as she pointed at Annie Mae and me.

José had just extracted all the information from Susie that we had tried to get. Except a clue. I asked, "What about your lipstick?"

"What?" Susie asked.

"The 'Back off Bert' message on her windshield." Annie Mae pointed at me. "With your lipstick. And Lucy's suicide note had the same lipstick."

"I only wrote the message on the glass. It washable and all," Susie stammered. "I just wanted you to leave Bert alone. You were bugging him. But I don't know anything about Lucy's note. I mean, I lost a tube at Bert's house. Maybe Lucy found it. I don't know."

José pulled out a pad from his shirt pocket. "So, you admit to vandalizing a car?"

"Oh, um. Yes. No. But...I..." Susie's neck turned red as she fidgeted with her necklace.

"So I can write up a report on these two for impersonating an officer." José motioned at Annie Mae and me as we stood side by side.

"Yes, yes. Do that." Susie nodded as she looked at José.

"Wait. I'm not done." José clicked his pen as he looked at Susie. "I can write up a report on you for vandalism."

Annie Mae whispered to me, "Now she's getting what's coming to her."

Susie fluttered her eyelashes at José. "Or why don't we just call it even and forget about everything?"

"Or you can just write the report on her." Annie Mae waved toward Susie.

"Humph." Susie glared at Annie Mae.

José furrowed his eyebrows and gave Annie Mae and me a twisted smile. "Are you sure you want to do that after what you two have done?"

"On second thought, forget all this ever happened," I added.

"Trust me. I won't forget all of it. There have been too many escapades recently." José closed his notebook. "And I'm hoping this is a lesson for those involved to stop."

CHAPTER 21

*A*nnie Mae and I were back in my SUV. "I propose we call it a day. We found out a whole lot of nothing."

"Today was a hoot, don't you think? And I got a new plant and a chandelier. To me, it's been a banner day."

"But we didn't solve anything." I turned onto Whitaker Street. "I just wish we could have figured out more than a bunch of random things."

"Pretty good for our first day as detectives."

"And our last. I feel like we just squandered our whole day."

"It's never a waste when you spend time with a friend." Annie Mae pulled out her cell. "It's almost eight."

"So?" I asked.

"We still could go over to Scarlett's store before it closes. Maybe she'll buy the chandelier. It kind of smells like smoke, but I'm sure that could be washed off."

I realized we were only a few blocks away. "I hope you make a small fortune from it."

"Wouldn't that be great?" Annie Mae grinned.

"Are you thinking that Lucy really killed herself?" I asked.

"No. Maybe. I don't know. Let's say that she found Susie's lipstick and was so heartbroken and distraught that she wrote the note with Susie's lipstick as a way to get back at Bert."

"I don't know. Although that's possible, it's hard for me to process. Mostly because she was fine when we saw her before she died. It still doesn't make sense to me." I took a left on Victory, passing the historic mansions lining both sides of the street. Branches from huge oak trees formed a canopy over the road. A few minutes later, I turned onto Habersham Street.

"It's hard for me to accept, too. But I think we're going to have to. Bert and Susie have alibis. Ina is also out as a suspect. The poor thing can barely hear, let alone commit murder. No one else had a motive." Annie Mae applied lipstick while looking in the passenger-side visor's mirror.

Driving down Habersham Street, I passed a variety of one- and two-story houses in Ardsley Park. "Our first official unofficial case is closed unsolved."

"There is still your dad's case."

"Yeah." I turned into the parking lot next to Blue Belle. "But I don't think we are any closer to solving that, either."

"Maybe when Micky calls, he'll have some information for you that may help."

"Fingers crossed." I parked and shut off the engine.

Annie Mae pulled hand sanitizer from her purse. She squirted some on her hands and then handed me the bottle. "Maybe this can help make me smell like lemons rather than burnt wood chips."

"Good idea. I doubt it will help much, but it's worth a try." I put a dab in my palm and rubbed it onto my hands. "Let's see how much your antique dumpster find is worth."

"I have a good feeling about it." Annie Mae unbuckled and got her chandelier.

I was disappointed that I had been wrong about Lucy being killed and me avenging her death. Maybe I had been wrong all along.

Perhaps it was suicide. That thought saddened me. I wished I'd known how desperate she must have felt. Maybe I could have prevented her death. Maybe I could have talked to her or gotten her help so that she didn't think death was her only option.

I sighed as I got out of my SUV. The air hung heavy with the remnants of the sticky, hot day. It smelled earthy from the rain earlier. Streetlights were on. Children giggled and chased each other near a group waiting outside an ice cream shop.

The sound of the chandelier clanging announced Annie Mae at my side.

"I'm thinking this is worth at least a thousand dollars. Do you think she'll throw in a candle, too?" Annie Mae asked.

"Sure. Why not?" I smiled. I did enjoy spending the day with Annie Mae. I'd had a day out with no children. Maybe it wasn't a total loss.

My phone rang; an unfamiliar number showed up.

"Hi, is this Catherine?" A shaky male voice was on the other end of the connection.

I held my hand up to Annie Mae as a signal to wait. We moved under a store awning. "This is Catherine."

"I'm Micky. I was a friend of your dad. I'm sorry about what happened to him."

"Me too. Thank you for calling me, Mr. Zwick. We stopped over earlier, and you were resting. Are you feeling any better?"

Annie Mae gave me a thumbs-up; apparently she heard that I was on the phone with Micky Zwick.

"Yes. Not as spunky as I was before, but I am doing just fine. Really, I feel pretty great."

"Good."

"Now what can I do for you? Karen said you had to ask me some questions? And please, call me Micky."

"Yes. I won't take up too much of your time. But I just wanted to know about the business you were in with my dad and a few others. It had something to do with junkyards and rebuilding cars?"

A long silence. Had I gotten disconnected? Glancing at my phone, I saw the call was still active.

"Mr. Zwick? Micky?" I asked.

Micky cleared his throat. "Yes. I'm still here. Catherine, that was a long time ago. We were friends and went into business together. Let's just say that, in the end, we decided it was best to dissolve the company and each go our own way."

"Did something happen to cause it to dissolve?" I asked.

"As I said, we all went our own way. We were all still friends. It's just that we knew the partnership would not work out." Micky's voice softened.

"Oh." I paused. "I don't know if you've heard, but three of your former business partners have died in the past two months. I don't know if there is any connection or not. I just had a hunch that maybe it had to do with something that happened when you were all working on the car business."

Silence.

"No. No connection that I know of. They were all good men. And it broke my heart to hear that they passed." Micky coughed.

"Okay. Well, I just thought that maybe there may have been a grudge or something that would cause someone to go after your group members."

"Listen, Catherine. We were all like brothers. None of us would ever do anything to hurt the other one." Micky cleared his throat. "If there is anything else you need, you can call me back. Listen, it's almost time for me to take my medicine."

"I'll let you go, then. Thank you for your time."

"Oh, Catherine, your dad was a good man. I need you to know that," Micky added.

Of course I knew that. Why did he feel he had to make a point to mention it? "Yes, I know. I miss him terribly."

"Well, then. Have a good day." Micky clicked off.

"So? What happened? I only heard your side of the conversation." Annie Mae and I continued along the sidewalk to Blue Belle.

"To sum it up—looks like a dead end. Micky doesn't think there are any connections with the deaths of his business partners, including my dad. He said they were all like brothers."

"Sorry, kiddo."

"There must be something else I'm missing," I said. "I wish I had gotten some sort of clue or something from Micky that would lead me to who shot my dad. Anything at all."

"At least you were able to talk to him."

"True."

"Is that Cowboy going into the store?" Annie Mae pointed as Cowboy entered Blue Belle.

"That's right. Scarlett asked him to come back at closing. I remember overhearing that he was picking up something from her." I opened the door and let Annie Mae walk in first. The bells let out a faint jingle. No one turned to look at us.

Upon entering, I saw Cowboy and Scarlett talking near the register. Scarlett's back was to us. I doubted she saw us.

Zachary approached. "Hi. Nice to see you again."

"Hi, Zachary." I shook his hand. "Do you know how long your aunt will be?"

"I'm not sure. She's with a client right now. I know he's important because she said that she cannot be disturbed, no matter what." Zachary scratched his neck. "And I don't want to make her mad."

"Oh?" Annie Mae's voice rose.

"She may be little, but she has a temper." Zachary looked down at his green gym shoes.

"I don't want to disturb her, either, but I've got this great chandelier that I think she'll love." Annie Mae held it up.

"It does look vintage," I added.

"And expensive, too," Annie Mae added. "This looks like something she could sell and make a whole lot of money."

"Maybe if I put it in the back room, I can have her look at it when she has a chance," Zachary said.

The bells on the door jingled. A couple pushing a stroller walked in.

"I have to help them." Zachary motioned to the customers.

"I could just put it back there myself," Annie Mae said.

"Only if that's okay with you?" I asked Zachary.

Zachary waved a hand. "Sure. Go ahead."

Annie Mae and I made our way to the back of the store.

Glancing over my shoulder, I saw Cowboy and Scarlett shaking hands. Seeing them together made me remember parts of their conversation this morning. An unsettling feeling rumbled inside me. "You know, something about Scarlett doesn't feel right."

"There's a lot not right. She's gotten a ton of surgical work done. I call that well-preserved. And trying to sell candles for a hundred bucks? Give me a break. That's not right." Annie Mae jiggled her chandelier.

"I was thinking about Scarlett and Cowboy's earlier conversation."

"Cowboy. Oh, baby, I think he's kind of cute. Tall and hunky."

"What about Tadcu?"

"He's a cutie, too. But I've got to keep my options open now that I'm out there dating again." Annie Mae circled her hand.

Pushing the thick tapestry curtain aside, we entered the back hallway. All the while, tidbits of conversations spun in my head. "Did anything strike you as odd about what Scarlett said to us earlier?"

Furrowing her brows, Annie Mae said, "Come to think of it, didn't she say something to the effect that Lucy had an accident? I mean, someone can slip and fall and accidentally kill themselves. But an accident with a butcher knife slitting a wrist? I don't think so."

"Right. I caught that as well. Although it may've just been a verbal slipup."

"Right." Annie Mae raised an eyebrow. "What else are you mulling over?"

"Now that we're back here, I'm thinking about Lucy's vase. Also, Cowboy had said to Scarlett how lucky she was she got something back." I shook my head. "None of this makes any sense. Just seems like a few pieces that don't fit."

Annie Mae peered in boxes. "Yeah, and remember how insulted Scarlett seemed to be when I told her I was surprised she sold such an ugly vase in her store?"

"Yes, the one in Lucy's house is rather run-of-the-mill, do-it-yourself pottery shop. But she'd shown me a picture of the room. I remember thinking it was a very pretty vase." I bent over, looking into a box.

"Then you need glasses."

"It's not adding up."

"You still have Lucy's cell phone, right?"

"Yes." I stood and looked at Annie Mae. "Why?"

"Following a hunch. We already looked at her texts and call log. I think we need to look at her pictures." Annie Mae set her chandelier down on a table.

"Good idea." I turned on Lucy's cell phone and began to look through her pictures.

Jazz music played as muted sounds of conversations came from the other side of the curtain that separated the back room where we stood from the showroom where Scarlett and Cowboy were. A strong scent of citrus hung in the air.

Annie Mae leaned over to see as I clicked though each picture on Lucy's cell. There were lots of photos of her cat and other pictures of animals. Some dozen or so pictures of her backyard garden were interspersed with several shots of the interior of her house.

"Stop. That's her sitting room." Annie Mae pointed.

I found the vase in the picture and enlarged it.

Annie Mae and I locked eyes.

"That is not the vase that is in her house now, that's for sure," Annie Mae said.

"Right. And I saw it somewhere else." A second later, I remembered. "The pattern along the top looks like the piece sticking out of a box back here."

"Holy smokes. You're right. What are you thinking?"

"Just that Lucy's vase may have been switched."

"By whom?"

"I don't know." I darted my eyes around, looking for the box I had seen earlier with the top of a blue-and-white porcelain item sticking out. I couldn't find it. Scarlett's office door was shut. I walked over and tried the door handle. Locked. I wondered if it was in there.

"I want to find out what Scarlett knew about the vase. Or if she knew someone who would have gone to Lucy's house to steal it."

"And switch it out." Annie Mae stood next to me trying the door handle. "Why is her door locked?"

"I don't know. But I wish I could figure out how to use my cell's recording device. I wanted my boys to teach me, but they never had the time."

"I know how to use mine."

"Great. Turn it on just in case something is said that could be used as evidence."

"Like?"

"I wish I knew. Let me call José." I tapped my speed dial. My battery was charged just enough for a quick call. "I'm calling José to tell him what we've found so far and to have him meet us over here."

"And do what?" Annie Mae leaned against a wall.

"I'm not sure. But I'm pretty sure the vase has something to do with Lucy's death."

José answered on the third ring. "Cat, what's going on?"

I got him up to speed then said, "It's almost closing time. I think Annie Mae and I have to break into Scarlett's office and find the vase."

"Hell no! Do not break in anywhere," José said.

I covered the cell phone and turned to Annie Mae. "He thinks it's a good idea."

Annie Mae's right eyebrow rose.

"I'll have to arrest you," José said. "Cat, are you still there?"

This time I had to go with my motherly instincts and not listen to logic. And my gut said to follow my hunch, even if that meant I had to betray my friend. But it was that important to find Lucy's killer. "Bad connection. Have to go now. Thanks, José." I ended the call.

"José really said that it was okay to break in? Let me talk to him. I don't think he's a rogue cop." Annie Mae pulled out her cell phone and tapped on it.

"Put that away." I took Annie Mae's phone and put it back in her purse. "Trust me. I know what I'm doing. We have to find the vase. I think it may be the key to something."

"Got you. You think that the vase may be evidence."

"Yes. At least I hope so. Let's catch a killer." The words stuck in my throat. I nervously twisted my dad's ring on my thumb.

"How?"

I jiggled Scarlett's office door handle. "First, we need to get in."

"Do we have to break in?" Annie Mae folded her arms on her chest. "Are you sure José said it was okay even after the whole deputizing thing?"

I gave a weak nod. A little white lie should be okay if it helped solve Lucy's death. "Any ideas on getting this door open?"

"In one of the plays I directed, we had to have an actor break into a locked door. So I did research on lock picking to make it look authentic. I might be able to get us in."

Annie Mae pulled a credit card and paper clip from her purse. She straightened the paper clip into a long piece of metal. She slid the credit card down the crack in the door next to the lock as she used her other hand to poke the metal into the lock. "We're in."

We entered the office. Luckily, no one was there.

Three sealed boxes sat on the table.

Annie Mae shrugged. "Now what?"

Quickly glancing around, I pointed to the boxes on the table. "We need to open them."

Annie Mae whispered, "What if we get caught? Sooner or later, someone is going to come back here. Zachary may wonder where we are. And what happens if Scarlett walks in?"

"If she sees us back here, we could just say we lost something earlier today when we were in her office."

"And we can tell her that the door was open already." Annie Mae gave a thumbs-up. "I'm getting good at this stealth investigating. Did you notice how I fibbed to Bert earlier, too, about the pictures on Lucy's cell phone?"

I heard a man's voice. I looked at my cell. It was seven fifty-five.

The man said, "Is it ready? I wired the first half of your money. The second half will arrive once I inspect it."

I put a finger to my lips and turned to Annie Mae. She

nodded. My head began to spin. "I'm getting scared now," I whispered.

"I'm right with you. It'll be okay." Annie Mae grabbed my hand and gave it a firm, quick squeeze. "Let's find that vase."

On my key chain, I had a pocketknife. I slid the knife along the seam and opened the first box. It contained a windup alarm and a red teakettle.

"Hey, this is the clock I wanted to buy. They didn't even call me first." Annie Mae held it.

"Focus. We are losing time." Opening the next box, I found an item padded in bubble wrap and newspaper. Pulling it out, I slowly took off the layers of padding, revealing a blue-and-white oriental porcelain vase.

"Whoa. Now that would've looked way better in Lucy's house." Annie Mae ran a finger over the vase. "Definitely old, but in pretty good shape."

My heart pounded so hard I was afraid that it was audible three blocks away. I felt Annie Mae's breath on my shoulder.

"I think this is Lucy's vase."

I set the vase on the table and pulled out Lucy's phone.

Scrolling through the photos stored on her phone, I found the one of her sitting room with the vase. Enlarging the picture, I held it next to the vase on the table.

"You're right." Annie Mae's eyes widened. "How did it get from her sitting room to here?"

"And replaced in her house by the other one?"

Outside the office, voices sounded like they were getting closer.

"Ms. Scarlett, I have to say, that vase is one of a kind," a deep male voice said.

"Yes." A woman let out a half laugh. "I was lucky, and now you are. Let's get your package, and you can be on your way."

"Let's find something right now to handcuff her." Annie Mae looked around and picked up packing tape from a worktable. "This will work."

"We can't do that. We still don't know what happened." I took the tape from Annie Mae and set it back on the table. "Although I think we need a serious talk with Scarlett. Is your recorder on?"

Annie Mae dug in her purse and held up her cell. She punched a button. "Secret spyware is on."

CHAPTER 22

*F*ootsteps came nearer. I jumped at the sound of the curtain's grommets sliding on the metal rod. Heavy thuds were followed by the sound of clicking heels.

Annie Mae and I exchanged a glance.

My hands shook. "It's Cowboy and Scarlett."

I grabbed my keys with my pocketknife. Annie Mae snatched the packing tape dispenser.

Scarlett walked into the office, followed by Cowboy.

Scarlett's eyes darted around, landing on the opened boxes. "How did you get back here?"

"You didn't see us? We walked right past you. You were busy talking." Annie Mae bit her lip.

She was getting good at lying, and so was I. Did all detectives have this talent to fib?

"Howdy, ladies. Nice to see you again." Cowboy smiled and tucked his hands in his jeans pockets.

"These two do not belong back here." Scarlett wagged a finger at Annie Mae and me.

Annie Mae lowered her voice. "Actually, we do, because we need to get something back that belonged to a friend of ours."

"There is nothing here that belongs to anyone but me." Scarlett shook a finger at us again.

"I beg to differ," Annie Mae said.

"We think we found evidence that you are in possession of Lucy's vase," I said.

"You two get out of here. Now." Scarlett held the door open.

"Whoa, now. These ladies aren't causing any trouble." Cowboy held a palm up. "Why don't I get the package so I can head out?"

I put my hand on top of the box. "I'm afraid you might not be able to do that."

"The vase belongs to someone else." Anne Mae stood next to me.

I patted the top of the box. "And it may be evidence in a murder."

"Hold on, there. Scarlett, is this true?" Cowboy glared at Scarlett.

"No." Shoving Annie Mae and me aside, Scarlett snatched the package. "These ladies just got out of the mental institution. I need to call their nurse."

"You want to see crazy? I'll go all crazy on your bony butt." Annie Mae lunged at Scarlett, but stopped short of hitting her. "You're lucky I have self-restraint."

"Don't mess me with, ladies. I'm calling the police." Scarlett turned to Cowboy. "Please don't worry about them. Everything is still okay with our transaction."

I held on to Annie Mae's arm and whispered to her, "What now?"

Annie Mae's voice deepened. "Scarlett. It's over. We know the truth. That vase belongs to Lucy, not you."

Cowboy frowned. "Ms. Scarlett, I'm a legitimate businessman and only do transactions that are fair and honorable. Since there's question about the vase's ownership, I'm afraid our deal is off. Good day, ladies." With that, he turned and marched out.

"Damn you two meddlers!" Scarlett turned red from her neck up to her face. She held the box close to her chest. "Why couldn't you have left well enough alone? This vase is worth millions."

"Holy cow." Annie Mae extracted the box from Scarlett. "I've never held millions. Did you find this in a dumpster?"

"You have made me madder than a hornet. I can't think straight." Scarlett dashed to the office door and locked it. "One thing for sure. You ladies are not leaving here alive."

"Huh?" My heart sank into my spinning stomach.

"You are so wrong, lady." Annie Mae held up the tape dispenser. "Don't come near me or else."

Scarlett opened a drawer and pulled out a gun. She shifted her gaze to me. Her hands shook as her eyes welled up with tears.

"Hey, put that thing away." Annie Mae held up a hand.

"We'll leave. You can have the vase," I offered.

"I ca-ca-can't," Scarlett stuttered.

"Sure you could. Here, just give me the gun. But like when you hold scissors, point it down to the ground before you hand it over." I held my hand out to Scarlett.

"Please," Annie Mae said. "You can stop all this nonsense now. Just put down the gun. We can work out this whole situation peacefully."

"No. I can't. You know too much." Scarlett held the gun in our direction.

Annie Mae said, "I'm forgetful."

"Trust me, so am I," I added. "So why don't we just leave you and your vase here? And we'll pretend like none of this ever happened."

"No. That won't work. I didn't want to hurt anyone. Now you put me in this awful situation. I am not a killer. I am a shop owner. I am a grandma." A tear ran down Scarlett's cheek.

"I believe you. I do," I offered.

"But now I am in this, and I have to finish it. I know what I have to do." Scarlett's voice quivered. Her eyes narrowed.

"Let us go, right?" Annie Mae grinned.

Scarlett's face tightened up. Her lips formed a thin line. "This is dripping with irony. Yes, I know who you are. I looked you up on the Internet after you left."

"Everyone knows Cat's family owns the Sunshine Market," Annie Mae said.

"I know." Scarlett shook the gun at me. "And after your dad was shot, I got the gun to protect myself at work. So, thanks to your dad, you now have a gun aimed at you."

My anger boiled in me as I clenched my fists. "Don't you even think about bringing my father into this."

Scarlett didn't have a clue that she'd just jammed a jagged knife in my open wound, talking about my father's death so casually. I was going to get out of here alive, or she was going down with me.

Annie Mae moved toward Scarlett. "Back off, bitch."

Scarlett cocked the trigger.

Annie Mae jumped.

"Here's the deal, ladies. That is my vase. It always was. And I will shoot you both and put the gun in your hand." Scarlett waved the gun at Annie Mae. "And claim you shot her, then yourself."

"Hey! Why do I have to be the killer?" Anne Mae said.

"Not important," I whispered to Annie Mae.

"But it is to me. I don't want people to think I'd shoot you." Annie Mae tapped her chest.

"It won't matter. You'll be dead." The corners of Scarlett's mouth curled like the Grinch's. "Plus, you have no proof that it was ever her vase."

Holding Lucy's cell phone up, I said, "You're wrong. I have proof."

Scarlett lowered her voice. "I'll just take that out of your cold, dead hands and destroy it."

"You sold it to her and then must have stolen it from her. What kind of operation are you running here?" Annie Mae flung her arms open, almost knocking over Scarlett's plant on her table. She grabbed the plant. "Sorry, JC."

"JC?" I asked.

"Jim Croce. I named it," Annie Mae said.

I turned back to the other woman. "So, Scarlett, tell us what happened."

"Stupid Zachary put the vase into the box. Idiot. That's what I get for hiring family. Stupid foo…fool," Scarlett faltered. "When I found out, it was too late. Lucy had already picked up the box."

"You knew its value, but Lucy didn't?" Annie Mae stared Scarlett down.

"She had no idea." Scarlett's lips tightened. "Imbecile."

"So you killed her to get it back?" I asked Scarlett.

"I mean, since you're going to shoot us, why not tell us the whole story? Then at least we can die in peace." Annie Mae fidgeted in her purse.

I hoped that she was making sure her phone recorder was on.

"Put your purse on the table. Now!" Scarlett glared at Annie Mae. "Do you think I'm stupid?"

"Well, since you asked, you are sort of a wackadoodle." Annie Mae slid her purse on the table and then put her hands up.

"You're wrong! I'm clever enough to find a vase worth millions." Scarlett's hand trembled.

"But then you sold it for a few bucks," Annie Mae pointed out. "So I'd say you were—"

"Shut up! Shut up!" Scarlett's neck flushed a bright crimson.

I could barely catch my breath. Scarlett had her back to the door and the gun pointed at Annie Mae and me. There were no windows and no other way out.

We were ensnared in this killer's potpourri-scented lair.

My only hope was that I had just called José, and he was on his way. I only hoped he got here before we were corpses. I shifted my stance, my legs buzzing with tense energy.

"By the way, nice little gun there. Is that a .38?" Annie Mae's voice was soothing and steady.

With one hand, Scarlett held the gun in our direction. The other hand she used to push a chair in front of the door.

Annie Mae slid a foot closer to Scarlett. "So, what happened with Lucy? Are you a cold-blooded killer, or what?"

Thank goodness she was doing the talking. I was so terrified

I heard my heart pounding in my ears. It seemed that the walls were closing in.

"No, I am not!" Scarlett waved both hands. Her voice softened. "She wasn't supposed to be home. She'd said she'd be out that night with her chubby club. But when I broke in, she was there."

I asked, "You went through the back window?"

"How did you know?" Scarlett's voice ascended.

"We have a witness."

"After all, we are detectives and did our investigation," Annie Mae added.

Of course, it was pure luck that we'd ended up back here. If Annie Mae hadn't found that chandelier in the dumpster and then decided to see if Scarlett wanted to buy it, we wouldn't have decided to return to Blue Belle. But I wasn't going to volunteer that information.

Annie Mae put her arm around my shoulder and then whispered in my ear, "Hang in there. We're going to be fine."

I gave her a weak nod. My legs felt rubbery and shaky. My teacher was right. Life was not fair. Lucy was dead, and now Annie Mae and I would be, too. While a killer was free.

"Then what took place once you got into her house?" Annie Mae asked.

"I don't know…it all happened so fast." Scarlett paced in front of the door, gun still in hand. "I'd surprised her. I tried to explain what was happening, but she was standing near knives, cutting up rolls. I grabbed the knife from her hand, but she fell back and hit her head. She wasn't breathing. I…I…I panicked."

"So you staged it to look like a suicide?" Annie Mae offered.

"I didn't know what else to do. I mean, I'm not a murderer. It was an accident." Scarlett's bottom lip quivered. "Really, it was. An accident. I didn't want to hurt anyone."

Poor Lucy.

Anne Mae leaned toward Scarlett. "You call stealing her vase an accident, too?"

"Um…" Scarlett stammered. "I was just swapping out one of Biddy's vases for Lucy's vase. It was fair."

Annie Mae flung her arms in the air. "Your granddaughter's vase for a million-dollar vase? That's hardly fair."

"But my Biddy's vase is priceless," Scarlett said.

Appealing to her maternal instincts and trying to get the aim of the gun away from us, I added, "I know what you mean. I think all of my children's artwork is priceless. And it is. So I know how you feel."

Scarlett seemed to relax her hand that held the gun. She slowly lowered it to her side. Her eyes welled up with tears. "It really was her best piece."

"Maybe to you. Not to anyone else," Annie Mae said. "Why didn't you just ask Lucy to give you the vase?"

"Lucy was such a sweet lady. And she liked you so much. I'm sure you could've worked something out." I positioned myself next to Annie Mae within clear sight of the only exit. Could we maneuver around Scarlett somehow and bolt toward the door?

"No one would hand over a multimillion-dollar vase that they paid hardly anything for." Scarlett stopped pacing. She pointed the gun back at us. "This has all gotten so mixed up. Now I have to kill you two. All I wanted was the vase. Not three dead people."

"Then how about you stop at one dead person?" Annie Mae suggested.

Scarlett's face softened into a smile, as if she was considering Annie Mae's suggestion. But then, in an instant, she hardened her face and fired in our direction.

We both ducked. The blast echoed in the room. The bullet hit a picture on the wall, shattering the glass.

"I take that as a no," Annie Mae said.

My heart beat so loudly that I thought I could hear it echoing off the office walls.

Annie Mae screamed, "Holy smokes, are you nuts, lady?"

My kids. My husband. I had to get out of this alive for them. I whispered to Annie Mae, "Self-defense time."

Years ago, José had taught me a self-defense move. I tried remembering the mechanics of it as I kicked my leg up, angling it toward Scarlett's hand holding the gun. Trying to sound tough, I added a fierce grunt with the kick.

Instantly, I lost my footing and slammed to the ground, hitting my butt bone.

Scarlett fired another shot. This time, the bullet hit a file cabinet. Thank goodness she was a crappy shooter.

"Are you okay?" Annie Mae scurried to me and held her hand out to pull me up.

"Yes." My tailbone throbbed as Annie Mae helped me to my feet.

"I got this." Annie Mae flung herself at Scarlett like a human wrecking ball, knocking the gun out of her hand. The gun slid under the table. I tried to figure out how to get it before Scarlett did.

Annie Mae pulled her shoulders back. "Self-defense, my ass. You just need bulk."

"You—you're crazy." Scarlett jumped on top of Annie Mae, knocking her to the ground.

Scarlett clung to Annie Mae's back. Seeing Annie Mae in trouble, I hopped on top of Scarlett. The three of us were stacked up like a monkey pile, all of our arms flailing and all of us screaming and grunting. Annie Mae freed herself from the pile. Scarlett twisted and grabbed my neck.

No one touches my neck.

Terror caused me to have tunnel vision. I pummeled Scarlett as I tried to get her hands off my throat. I grabbed her hair. A huge chunk came out in my hand. It was a scratchy, tangled, brunette mess that smelled of hair spray.

Hair extension? I tossed it aside.

Scarlett's hands were soft and tiny, but they had a vise hold on my neck. I sucked in a breath but couldn't swallow or speak.

Scarlett and I flipped over. I gasped for air.

The suffocating sensation overcame me. I felt lightheaded and faint.

Righting herself, Annie Mae yanked Scarlett's hands away from my neck.

"You're a powerful little thing, aren't you?" Annie Mae held

Scarlett's arms behind her back. "Do you get strength injections with all that Botox?"

Scarlett let out a bloodcurdling scream. "Bitches!"

"Now, now. I suggest you keep your mouth shut. If you don't, you will see me go crazy all over you." Annie Mae tightened her grip on Scarlett and panted. "And by the way, you don't deserve to own a plant, so I'm taking yours to keep mine company."

Sweat drenched my shirt. I was shaking as I stood, rubbing my backbone. I put my hand on Annie Mae's arm. "Thanks for getting her off me."

The door flew open, knocking over the chair. José ran in, gun drawn. "Freeze!"

Annie Mae kept a hold of Scarlett, both of them huffing.

Scarlett's dress was hiked up, one of her shoes was off, and her hair, what was left of it…well, not so pretty.

I pointed at Scarlett, gasping. "She killed Lucy."

"Everyone stand still. Line up against that wall facing me. Hands visible." José lowered his gun. "I need to hear what is going on, right now."

We lined up against the back wall. Scarlett stood, back against the wall, straightening her dress.

"Scarlett is a killer. She has Lucy's vase." Annie Mae waved her phone in the air. "You heard it all, didn't you?"

José held his palm facing us. "Most of it."

"He did?" I asked Annie Mae.

"I didn't have time to set up the recorder, so I just hit José's number."

"Good job." I high-fived Annie Mae.

Scarlett held her chin up high and kept her mouth shut and her eyes on Annie Mae.

As we finished retelling José the story, Annie Mae said, "Thanks for letting us break in, or we would've never figured it out otherwise."

"Letting you break in?" José stared at me and then at Annie Mae. "I approved no such thing."

I held my thumb and forefinger close together. "Maybe I told a little white lie."

"You need to arrest them. They've just admitted to a crime." Scarlett thrust a bony finger at Annie Mae and me.

"I don't think you're in a position to point fingers." Annie Mae went nose to nose with Scarlett. "You're a murderer."

"You're a criminal and a pain in the ass." Scarlett leaned in, almost touching Annie Mae.

To avoid a fight, I moved between them. I didn't want Annie Mae getting hurt. I looked at José. "Sorry about the little white lie."

José sucked in deep breath and looked at me. "I'll deal with you later."

"Arrest them for breaking into my office." Scarlett ran over to José.

My heart raced as I spit out, "Then arrest her for murder and theft and… and…"

"Overuse of plastic surgery," Annie Mae added.

"What?" Scarlett bolted toward Annie Mae.

José held an arm up and stopped Scarlett in her tracks.

"Sorry. But, really, just look at her face. There's a lot of fillers in there." Annie Mae shrugged.

Scarlett stomped her foot. "I need my lawyer. Now."

José read Scarlett the Miranda rights, then cuffed her. After he called his precinct, he turned to Annie Mae and me. "Good job solving the murder. But about the matter of breaking in…"

CHAPTER 23

*B*ezu placed a ladle in the chili. Next to the pot of chili was a plate stacked with cornbread. A container with butter sat next to a glass pitcher of iced tea. "I don't want this conversation to get as ugly as ten miles of bad road, but we have to talk about how y'all almost got killed trying to be detectives."

"We were on our first case. And it was quite a success." Annie Mae spread a hunk of butter on top of her cornbread and then poured chili on top.

"I wouldn't exactly say that." José stretched his arms behind his head.

"But we caught a killer. It doesn't matter how we went about it, right?" I filled my glass with iced tea.

"It does." José let out a deep breath. "Where do I begin? You committed several felonies. Including breaking and entering."

"Scarlett's office?" Annie Mae asked.

"And trespassing," José said.

"Where?" I asked.

"The construction dumpster is not public property, and you two entered it, then nearly got fried. Let's just say there were a slew of wrongs."

"Oh." Annie Mae looked down at her plate.

José leaned his elbow on the table. "Impersonating an officer."

"I forgot about that." Annie Mae put a bite of food in her mouth. "We couldn't really hear your answer because of a siren, so I can claim that as just a miscommunication."

José continued, "And committing fraud."

"We never did that." I picked up my fork.

"Not you, exactly. But our resident actress. Remember the fall in the Red and White?" José twisted a grin as he inclined his head toward Annie Mae.

"It wasn't like we were trying to extract money from anyone. We were just trying to get information." Annie Mae wiggled her fork in the air. "And we succeeded."

José reached over, plucked a piece of cornbread, and put it on his plate. "What I'm trying to say is I love you girls, and you almost got yourselves killed. Putting yourself in danger is inexcusable."

"We never thought we'd end up with a gun pointed at us. Scarlett seemed so prissy. Who knew she was packing?" Annie Mae held her hands up.

I shrugged. Andrew and my mom were sick at the thought of someone with a gun aimed at me. However, they were glad we'd avenged Lucy's death and that Annie Mae and I were safe.

Bezu straightened her back in her chair. "I agree with José. You two were not using the good sense God gave you."

"And that needs to be the end of whatever that was." José held the palm of his hand facing us.

"But we put a murderer behind bars." Annie Mae put another spoonful of chili in her mouth.

"Breaking the law is breaking the law. Thankfully, you don't have any charges against you. I'm sure if it was anyone else but me coming to your rescue at Susie's house, you would have been taken into custody." José buttered his cornbread.

"That would have been a hoot if we were thrown in jail—even better, in the same cell as Scarlett." Annie Mae wiped her mouth with the linen napkin. "I can't wait to visit her in a few months."

"She's a murderer. Why in the Lord's name would you want to see her?" Bezu asked.

"Not her per se. Her face. Can you imagine what she will look like after a few months with no cosmetic injections and such? I bet she will age ten years in the span of a few weeks." Annie Mae giggled. "That I want to see."

"The judge is setting her bond today. With all the evidence, she should be in jail a long time," José said.

"Wasn't it cool, too, that the vase turned out to be from the Ming Dynasty?" I tore off some of my cornbread and then plopped it into my mouth.

"The Ming Dynasty. Absolutely amazing," Bezu said.

"Once the news showed a picture of the vase, a museum expressed interest in purchasing it. It's worth over twenty million," Annie Mae said.

"You can't make that kind of money in fifty lifetimes." José shook his head.

I added, "Even better, if they acquire the vase, they would have a plaque displayed next to it with Lucy's name in her memory."

"Now that is super neat." Annie Mae put her napkin on the table.

"Best of all, after taxes, the money will be split between Lucy's church and the humane society, per Lucy's will. And she ended up leaving them way more than she ever thought, not knowing about the vase and all," I said.

"That cheating scum, Bert, was left with the house." Annie Mae scowled. "Too bad he got anything."

"Good or bad, he was her husband," Bezu said. "So he should have been left something."

"A pile of garbage would have been better," Annie Mae argued.

"The Blue Belle Antique Shoppe is temporarily closed, although I heard rumors that Zachary's family wants to buy it and let him run it," I said.

"He's a sweet kid. I bet he'll do a great job," Annie Mae said. "I wonder if he could get me the silver windup clock and candle?"

"I'm sure he could." I grinned.

"Looks like we made the front page of the newspaper, our pictures and a great article and all." Annie Mae slid the *Savannah Morning News* to me as we sat around Bezu's dining room table. "I think I should've at least gotten that hundred-dollar candle as a reward. But I did take her plant I named JC. After all, I couldn't let him die in her office. Plus, my plant Marvin Gaye needed a friend."

I grinned. "Solving Lucy's murder was reward enough for me."

Bezu looked at the newspaper. "You're celebrities. What a good photo of both of you."

"You did take a great picture," José added.

"I do photograph well." Annie Mae patted her hair. "Now I have so many people calling me, acting like I'm the queen bee of Savannah. It's great. This has to be a boon for my dating life. Speaking of dates, Tadcu is picking me up for the movies soon. I think your mom is coming with. She wants to see the movie, too."

"Good. They really think you and I are quite the team. And my girls absolutely loved that I solved a crime like Nancy Drew." I smirked. "To them, I'm a hero."

"What about the boys?" Bezu asked me.

"They thought the whole episode was kind of cool. Except for the gun pointing at me. We didn't tell the girls about the gun. They'd have nightmares, mostly because of what happened to their grandfather." I filled my glass with iced tea.

"No kidding. It gave me nightmares thinking of you and Annie Mae putting yourselves in such danger." Bezu wrung her hands. "Don't ever go and do that type of fool thing again. Y'all acted like you had no sense."

José cleared his throat. "They sure stirred up the city. Getting stuck in a burning dumpster will go down in our unofficial police department history book of stupid people predicaments."

Looking over at me, Annie Mae lifted an eyebrow and smiled. "José, I have no idea what you're talking about."

José stood and stretched his arms. "You know exactly what I'm talking about."

"Fine," I said to José. "So maybe we did have a slightly unorthodox way of going about the investigation. We got the job done. And that's what counts."

"I agree," Annie Mae said. "We made a great team and put a killer behind bars."

I sipped on my iced tea. The cool, lemon-infused liquid tasted great.

"I'm just glad that your makeshift detective days are over," José said.

"Andrew and Tadcu feel the same way you do, José." I chuckled. "My mom, well, she just rattles off stuff in Korean at me while shaking her hands. Which I think means that she's happy I'm safe but thinks I was crazy getting involved."

Although I still grieved for Lucy and my father, I knew at least Scarlett was paying for her crime. My dad's murderer was still out there, but I felt that finding the second crossword puzzle meant I was somehow closer to finding my father's killer.

The doorbell rang. Bezu let in Tadcu and Yunni.

Yunni wore white capris and a blue sleeveless top, her hair up in a loose bun. Tadcu wore a pressed white short-sleeved shirt and khaki slacks. His hair was slicked back.

We all said our hellos.

"We're a little early. I hope we didn't interrupt anything," Tadcu said.

"Not at all. We were just having some chili and catching up. Please, join us." Bezu lifted two plates.

"No, thank you. I already ate. Also, I want to get ice cream at Leonardo's after the movie." Yunni winked. "So I could check in on grandson, too."

"Mom, I don't think Timmy needs any checking up on, but I know he'd love to see you." I took a sip of tea.

"Oh, here is extra paper for you. Nice picture of both of you." Yunni waved the paper at Annie Mae and me.

"Thanks." I took the paper from my mom and put it in my purse.

"I've got to go. It was nice seeing everyone again." José looked at Annie Mae and me. "No more breaking and entering."

"We actually didn't break anything. But we did enter and look. No crime in that." Annie Mae tapped José on the arm. "Right?"

My phone signaled a text. I read it out loud: "Dog lost. Can the Chubby Chicks Club find him for me? I will pay big money."

José stood and put his hands in the air. "I'm out of here."

Bezu shook her head and walked out of the room.

Tadcu and Yunni both stared at Annie Mae and me as though we had lost our minds.

Annie Mae said, "What type of dog and how much?"

I shrugged. "I guess it wouldn't hurt to call them back, huh?"

CHAPTER 24

*A*s I left Bezu's house, I pulled the paper out of my purse. On opening the story about Annie Mae and me solving Lucy's murder, I saw the headline next to our story. *Prominent Lawyer, M. Zwick Dies.* My heart skipped a beat.

I sat down on Bezu's front step and read the story. I had just talked to him the other day. He'd said that he was fine. I felt an overwhelming need to go over and pay my respects; after all, he'd said that he and my father were like brothers.

I went to my house and grabbed a sympathy card. Since I lived close by, I decided to hand-deliver the card.

Fifteen minutes later, I stood at Micky's front door. I rang the bell.

The door opened.

Karen, her eyes red, was dressed in black. "Hi. Catherine, right?"

"Yes. I just found out about Micky. I am so sorry."

"Please come in." Karen led me into the front sitting room. Vases of flowers adorned tabletops. A side table held a stack of papers and cards. It smelled of flowers and coffee.

"Can I get you anything?" Karen asked.

"No, thank you. I just came by to pay my respects. I am so sorry."

"We all are. Micky was one of a kind." Karen's eyes welled up.

"I just spoke with him the other day, and he said he was fine."

"I know. He was. It all happened so suddenly. I feel it's all my fault." Karen wrung her hands.

"Why?"

"I left him alone for an hour. He told me to go. He said that he was going to sleep. That I didn't need to keep tabs on him," Karen said.

"Uh-huh."

"He told me that he really didn't need twenty-four-hour care. His doctor even said I needn't be here all the time. I just…I have been a part of the family for so long. I raised all his children. I was with him when his wife died. I—I mean…" Karen looked at me with pleading eyes.

"You had a special relationship?" I offered.

"Yes. Yes. I loved him." A tear spilled down Karen's cheek.

I put an arm around her shoulder. "I am so sorry."

"I don't understand. He was fine when I left. We had gotten out for a walk around the park. We'd even stopped for lunch. It was really one of his better days," Karen said between sobs.

She continued, "It doesn't make sense. I had to run to the grocery store before it closed. He likes their organic dates and their peaches. It's right around the corner by the park."

"The Sunshine Market?"

"Why, yes, you know the store?"

"My folks own it."

"He just loves your store." Karen sucked in a breath. "I mean loved. It seems surreal that I am talking about him in the past tense."

"After my dad was killed, I still caught myself talking about him in the present tense."

"I don't know how I'm going to make it through this."

"It'd be great if there were a pill or a spell of some sort that could wipe away all the pain and grief. Right?"

Karen nodded as she wiped her cheek with the back of her hand.

"I can't tell you how many times I catch myself wanting to

talk to him or enter the store thinking that I'd see him in his yellow apron stocking produce." I felt the tug at my heart.

"Can I be frank with you?"

"Sure."

"Losing the one you love, well, it sucks."

I let out a long breath. "Yes, it does."

The doorbell rang.

Karen reached for my hand. "Thank you, Catherine, for listening to me. I am sorry I spilled my sorry sob story on you."

I held her hand for a second. "No problem."

"Please, excuse me." Karen left to answer the door. "You are welcome to stay. There are food and beverages in the kitchen. Please help yourself."

"Thanks."

Deciding it was time to leave, I retrieved the sympathy card from my purse and set it on top of the pile of papers on the sideboard.

As I turned, my purse knocked down the stack, scattering it to the ground. I knelt down to pick up the sprawling mess.

I gathered cards, letters, newspapers, and magazines addressed to Micky Zwick or Resident. One part of a newspaper was folded over. Opening the fold, I saw it was the crossword puzzle.

My breath caught in my chest as I read the purple-inked squares that said, "Got You."

THE END

MURDEROUS MUFFINS (BOOK 2)

Bezu is a beautiful southern belle with genteel manners. Her problems, however, are anything but. Deep in debt, Bezu's illegally taken in a few lodgers: A sweet stripper and her body-builder boyfriend, an Asian man loudly learning English through pop music, and a mysterious stranger with the most amazing blue-green eyes—and a secret. But when one of the boarders dies—with her muffins used as the murder weapon—Bezu must catch the killer before she ends up in jail…or worse.

Murderous Muffins **is now available in eBook, paperback, and audiobook.**

CHAPTER 1

The oven's digital temperature flashed zeros.

"Doggone thing could make a preacher cuss." I yanked out the muffin pan and slammed the oven shut. Setting the pan on the cooling rack, I poked a toothpick in the top of one of the chocolate-chip treats. Dry. Praise the Lord, at least they'd finished cooking before the oven went out again. The switch probably needed to be rewired.

"Good thing you learned some fixer-upper techniques from YouTube," I told myself.

Continuing my morning routine, I reached in the refrigerator, which thankfully still worked, pulled out a glass pitcher of orange juice, and placed it on the table. After pouring the freshly brewed coffee into a warming carafe, I set out cups, glasses, silverware, and small plates. I placed crisp white linen napkins near the flowered heirloom dishes and rearranged the blue hydrangeas in the crystal vase in the center of the kitchen table. After straightening the yellow lace tablecloth to smooth out any wrinkles, I lined up the glasses and cups.

Before my boarders woke, I returned to the walk-in pantry—which doubled as my makeshift bedroom. I gathered the tattered quilt and threadbare blanket. Folding the blanket, I set it on the small cot with the paper-thin mattress and placed my pillow on top of the pile. Closing the pantry door, I looked around my sunny yellow kitchen with ten-foot ceilings, splinter cracks in the plaster, and worn whitewashed pine cupboards that stretched high above gray-speckled Formica countertops. As I walked, the heart pine floors creaked, a comforting sound that brought me back to my childhood. Hide-and-seek had had its challenges then because the seeker could always hear the telltale squeak in the floorboards, and the hider would be discovered in short order.

Throughout my youth, I'd considered this house a castle, with me as the resident princess. With the help of my nanny, Hattie, I'd named our home Amia, which meant "beloved."

Sighing aloud, I put my hand on a yellow plaster wall as I rubbed my fingertips along the rough and brittle peeling paint. As a child, I'd taped my drawings on the very same wall. Every inch of this house seeped with memories of the generations of Gordons who had once lived here. Sometimes I could close my eyes and hear laughter floating from the sitting room, where my parents and grandparents had spent countless hours entertaining friends, family, and other visitors. The parlor was where Hattie and I would stay up late at night watching old movies, memorizing our favorite lines. "Amia, you are all I have left of my family, even if you're falling apart. I'll keep us together. I promise."

A quote from Citizen Kane popped into my head: "I can remember everything. That's my curse, young man. It's the greatest curse that's ever been inflicted on the human race: memory." How true that was.

The doorbell chimed. Who could that be at 7:00 a.m.? Taking a quick glance at my reflection in the silver teakettle, I smoothed my flyaway blond hair and straightened the bow on my pale blue sundress. Good enough for this early in the morning.

Upon opening the door, I saw my dear friend, Cat. Even at this hour, she looked adorable. Her pale skin and dark hair made her white teeth look even brighter. Half Korean and half Caucasian, Cat stood about five foot six, a few inches shorter than me. At forty, and after her two sets of twins, she had a remarkably cute figure.

I stood five foot ten, slender, with wispy, shoulder-length blond hair and green eyes, quite a contrast to Cat's dark hair and more athletic build. Sometimes I envied Cat. Her husband, Andrew, adored her and had to be the nicest guy this side of the Mason-Dixon Line. My only luck attracting men seemed to be men of the bad variety.

A suitcase stood next to her. Was she heading to the airport? "Good morning." I tried to hold down the confusion in my voice for fear of sounding rude. "How lovely to see you."

A strand of Cat's hair fell across her eyes. "Bezu, I'm sorry about the early hour and all, but I knew you'd be up."

"Please, come in. Would you like some breakfast? I have fresh muffins."

"It smells great in here. Like my mom's kitchen when she gets in the baking mood."

"Hattie used to say, 'A home is warmed by love and what is baking in the oven.' Let me get you something to eat." I then asked, "Are you going somewhere? I don't want to keep you from anything."

"Like what?"

"Your flight? Or travel plans?"

Cat tilted her head. "Why do you think that?"

"You have a suitcase. I thought that perhaps you were on the way to the airport." Always glad to help a friend, I added, "I'd be glad to give you a ride if you need one."

"No. Not going anywhere too far." Cat's eyes were puffy, as if she hadn't slept. "I sort of moved out of my house."

"Oh, my." My heart sank for her. She and Andrew had been married over twenty years. Was there something wrong with her marriage? "Moved out?"

Dread overcame me. As much as I loved her, I hoped she wasn't going to ask to stay here. My house was full. And then there was my secret. It was all too complicated.

"It's only temporary." Cat picked up the suitcase and followed me back to the kitchen. She plopped down in a chair.

Thinking of Cat moving out of her beloved home caused a

viselike grip in my gut. I hoped that she was okay. Pouring two cups of coffee, I set one down in front of her.

Poor thing. "I don't mean to pry, but what's going on? I'm assuming that something not so great happened at your house?"

Cat sighed. "It's tricky."

"If you don't want to talk about it, that's okay."

"No. I mean, I'll talk. It's not that things are bad. It's just that they aren't right, either. That's the reason I left."

I pulled a chair up to the table and sat next to her. "Oh?"

"You see, my mom took the girls to Korea, and Andrew and Tadcu went with them. My mom and dad took the boys when they were the same age. Of course, they wanted me to go, too, but no way was I going. I put my foot down and said no one should go, not after my dad got killed."

"Your dad died here, not in Korea."

"I know." Cat shook her head. "It's weird, but I have this feeling that it's not safe if we're not together, keeping an eye out for each other."

"You mean, it's not safe if you can't keep a constant vigil over everyone. Which means keeping them all here under your watchful eye?"

"Hmph." Cat grabbed a muffin and tore off a piece.

I reached over and placed my hand on top of hers. "Cat, I'm sorry about what happened to your dad."

Cat nodded, looking at me with watery eyes. She turned a ring on her thumb. "I need to stay in Savannah and find his killer. It's hard to explain, but somehow I feel that I'd lose momentum if I stopped now."

"You still think it was murder and not just a botched robbery like the police said?"

"Yes." Cat's deep brown eyes widened. "And I'm getting so close to finding out what really happened that night."

"How so?"

"Remember that his former business partner, Micky Zwick, died suddenly as well. That makes three dead partners, who all had crossword puzzles with messages in purple ink left near their corpses. That's gotta mean something."

"Like what?"

"A clue." Cat shrugged. "I'm not sure. But the trail is hot. I can't leave it. Not now." Cat leaned in, closer to the table. "Also, I have boxes in my SUV. I've wanted to go over some accounting stuff for Sunshine Market. We have so much to take care of now that my dad is gone, and it's too much for my mom to do. So you see, I have way too much to do here. I just couldn't go with them."

"I see." I nodded halfheartedly, not really understanding her reasoning for staying here when she could be on vacation with her family. But I cherished her and wanted to be supportive.

Cat twisted her mouth as though deep in thought. "And my house is so eerie now that it's empty. I can't sleep there."

I felt bad for her. She seemed so lost.

Cat unfolded a napkin. "So, I came here."

Uh-oh. I wanted so badly to offer her a place to stay, but then she'd find out what I had tried to hide from her and the rest of the Chubby Chicks Club. They couldn't know that I was illegally taking in boarders. I could get in all sorts of financial and legal trouble. Not that they would tell anyone, but once it was out of the bag, who knew who might find out? I had a pile of letters from the IRS and needed the tenants' rent money in order to keep the house from being taken away.

How did I tell a friend—whom I would do anything for—that she couldn't reside with me? At least not now. I'd be humiliated if she knew that I'd run out of money, was close to bankruptcy, and was teetering on the edge of losing my house. Maybe she wouldn't ask me, although she had shown up at my doorstep with her luggage. So it was only a matter of time.

I fidgeted with my hair. "It's nice out today. Don't you think? Not too stiflingly humid, as it has been. I think it'll be a perfect day."

"Yes." Cat gazed at me as she sipped her coffee. "I really don't want to bother you, but I'd like to ask you something." She set her cup down and looked inside it.

"Oh?" Perhaps her cup was empty. I picked up the carafe. "Do you need more? Here, let me top you off."

Cat put her hand over her cup. "No. I'm fine. But thanks."

"Was there something else?"

Cat played with the saucer under her cup. She moved it from side to side. "You see, I was thinking about the Chubby Chicks Club. And I thought... Well, I don't know how to say this."

"What?"

Cat gazed at the flower centerpiece. "Um, well, never mind."

Maybe she didn't want to stay here after all. "Speaking of our little group, what are Annie Mae and José up to? I haven't seen them in a while."

"Annie Mae is away on an exchange professor teaching assignment at UNC Chapel Hill."

"Is that so? She's still working? She had mentioned retirement."

"Yes, she plans on leaving her job soon, but not yet." Cat grinned. "She loves to keep busy. I tell you what, she had so much fun playing detective on Lucy's case with me, I think if she had a chance, she would do it again. As for me, trying to find out what happened to my dad, keeping my family safe, and running the business are enough. I don't need to get involved in sleuthing."

"Although, I was very proud of how you and Annie Mae found out who killed Lucy," I said.

Cat smirked. "I have to admit, I kind of liked being a hero for the day and putting the killer behind bars."

"That was great. The whole city is still talking about it, too. You and Annie Mae were celebrities." I sipped my coffee. "Who knew a sweet, rather upstanding store owner could commit murder?"

"I know. People never fail to surprise me."

"You're right about that."

"I'm glad that whole detective thing is done and behind me. Anyway, Annie Mae is out of town. She invited me to go up to North Carolina with her. But I said that I needed to stay in Savannah. Keep my eye on things here." Cat's shoulders sagged. "I'd like to talk to her, but she said she's going to be out of touch for a few days as well. We'll see her soon enough, not that anything exciting is going to happen around here that she'll miss."

"No kidding. It's pretty lackluster around here." I asked, "So, I've been out of the loop for a few days—what's going on with José?"

"He's showing some new police recruits the ropes."

"Good. It never hurts to have more law enforcement on the streets." I fidgeted with my cup. "Does he still play poker?"

Cat nodded. "All the time. He told me that he won big the other night."

"He's lucky."

"Well, I'm not so sure about that. He keeps winning against his archrival, Officer Ray Murphy."

"Yes, I remember him. We met him the day we found Lucy." My heart sank as I thought back to when all of us had found Lucy on the floor of her house, wrist slit open.

Cat paused for a moment. "I still can't believe that she's gone."

"Me, either." My eyes welled up. "But we still have each other."

"I am so thankful for all of you." Cat put her hands in prayer formation.

"Me, too. The Chubby Chicks Club is my family."

"Speaking of family, now that mine are out of town, actually out of the country, I'd like to find a place to stay so I won't be alone."

The back of my throat tickled. I let out a small cough. "Any place in mind?"

"José has an extra room at his house, but forget that. A married woman like me at a hunky single guy's place just wouldn't do." Cat's dark brown eyes shifted up.

I leaned forward in my chair. "But he's not interested in women."

Cat grinned as we locked eyes. "You, Annie Mae, and I know that, but no one else does. It could cause a scandal."

"You're right. You know what they say about Savannah: 'If you don't know what you're doing, someone else does.'"

"Did Hattie say that?" Cat smiled.

"She had more Southern expressions than there are azaleas in Savannah." Because of my frequent use of Southernisms, Cat and Annie Mae kidded me that I spoke another language. "But you won't be by yourself. Aren't your boys still home?"

"Nope. They're spending a few days at a friend's Tybee beach house. I'm solo." Cat tapped the table.

"You have me."

"I know. But I don't want to impose on you."

"You know that you're always welcome here. It's just that I have a new tenant—I mean, relative—arriving today. He's staying in the last open bedroom. So it's not like I don't want to offer you a place to stay, it's just that I don't have a suitable room for you. I'd want you to be comfortable."

"Oh, please don't worry about having something elaborate for me. I'm not picky. I can take the couch." A smirk crept onto Cat's face. "With four kids, you know I can fall asleep standing up if I have to. I don't want to be alone at my house or in a hotel room." Cat pushed her plate away from her.

Folding a linen napkin, I thought of all the reasons I should refuse her. As much as I treasured Cat, my little world felt like only duct tape and a prayer held it together.

I took a deep breath. *Say no. Say no.* "Why, I insist that you stay here."

Cat jumped out of her chair and flung her arms around my neck as she gave me a quick peck on my cheek. "Are you sure? You're the best."

"You're always welcome, Cat."

Cat sat back down. "Thanks."

Footsteps thumped on the wood floor. Mr. Phong, one of my longtime boarders, who everyone believed was a very distant relative, entered the kitchen singing, "Everybody, let's get up. Hey, hey. Hey, hey. Hey, hey. If you can't hear what I am a-saying, then read my paper."

At sixty-something, he'd learned English by singing pop songs, at least his version of the songs. This one sounded like Robin Thicke's "Blurred Lines."

"Good morning, Mr. Phong, do you remember my friend Cat?"

Mr. Phong, wearing a tweed suit and a pressed, green cotton shirt, nodded and grinned from ear to ear. A headphone cord dangled from each ear. "Maybe I am out of the mind."

Cat grabbed and shook Mr. Phong's hand. "Nice to see you again. It looks like we're going to be housemates for a while."

Mr. Phong shrugged his shoulders as he continued to sing. As he waved his hand, I saw the flash of his ruby-and-diamond ring. He poured a glass of juice and grabbed three muffins before he exited the kitchen.

I made a dozen muffins every day, but Mr. Phong always took a few to start and then came back later to get whatever was left. At least they never went to waste.

"You told us, but I forgot. How's he related to you?" Cat stood.

Rats. What had I told her before? I got up, then glided my chair in. "My brother-in-law's third cousin, twice removed."

Cat set her coffee cup in the sink. "He's getting better with English."

"Yes, he is. It's all that listening to pop songs. And singing out loud, really loud."

"Does that get on your nerves?"

"Not mine. I can tune it out pretty well. Although I'm not sure how my other guests feel about it. But that's a part of living together. We have to accept each other's idiosyncrasies."

"How many relatives do you have staying here now?"

My eyebrows rose. With Cat around, I'd have to call them relatives and not boarders. "Two: Mr. Phong and a sweet young college student, Lily. Well, and her boyfriend practically lives here, too. So, actually that makes three."

"How is Lily related?"

Think. Think. "My great-great-aunt's sister-in-law's step niece. Or something along those lines." I'd never remember all the tales I'd spun. I just hoped Cat would forget them, too. "Oh, and there is one more guest due to arrive today. He's some sort of temporary contractor here to work at that new company on Bay Street."

"It has initials, I think one is S and stands for Souza?"

"Yes, that one."

"Sounds like you'll have a full house." Cat washed her cup and put it on the drying rack.

I only had one decent bedroom left, but it was reserved for the new tenant. The only other bedroom upstairs was mine, and it had a collapsed ceiling corner due to a leak, which, in turn, had soaked the wood floor beneath it. That was why I slept in the walk-in pantry. I simply hadn't had the time or the funds to fix the leak. I'd had to discard the bed because it was soaked through. Luckily, the dresser and nightstand were still intact.

Now that Cat was here, I needed to make the room livable on a dime. And pray that it didn't rain, for I feared that she'd be washed out of the room. After I quickly catalogued what I had in my backyard shed, I came up with some things that might work. I'd nail a sheet of plastic to the ceiling and cover the damaged floor with a piece of plywood, then throw a rug over that so Cat wouldn't get splinters. There was an old collapsible cot that could work as a rather decent bed. I'd have to figure out how to fix the folding leg on the cot to make sure it didn't crumple on Cat.

"I really appreciate you letting me stay here. Thank you." Cat dried her hands on a floral kitchen towel. "I don't want it to be too much for you."

"Don't be silly."

"So you're sure it's no trouble?"

"None at all." Having her in my home created a pail full of difficulties for me, but I'd sell my soul to help Cat. "I'll put you upstairs in the corner bedroom."

"Wait." Cat held up her hand. "As I remember, you only have four bedrooms, and that one is yours. I'll crash somewhere down here. I don't want to take your room."

"No, you will not. I have a few things to fix up first. But I insist you take the bedroom."

"Where will you sleep?"

The walk-in pantry. Like I've slept in for weeks now. "Don't worry about me. I have a cozy place to sleep downstairs." And that was the truth.

Cat picked up her suitcase. "This will be fun."

This might turn into a nightmare, but my dear friend needed me. "It sure will be."

"I'll just put my things in the room. Then I have to go to the Sunshine Market and check up on our assistant manager. While I'm there, I'll get us some groceries. What do you think about Mexican tonight?"

"Lovely," I said.

"Then that is what we'll have." Cat walked up the stairs.

The doorbell chimed.

I opened the door to find a slim, dark-haired man on my porch. His eyes were a deep blue-green, his smile full of straight white teeth. Dimples formed in his cheeks, and his skin was deep golden-brown, as though he was of Latin descent.

My, oh, my. He looked like a tall, cool drink of tequila.

A guitar and a large, beige duffle bag stood next to him. He wore a white T-shirt, a beige linen blazer, and snug faded jeans with cowboy boots.

He stuck out his hand. "I'm Xavier, your new tenant."

Murderous Muffins is now available in eBook, paperback, and audiobook.

ACKNOWLEDGMENTS

Any story starts with an idea and then grows from there. Along the way, many people helped and supported me as I turned my idea into a finished book. First and foremost, thanks go out to my husband, Tom, and our fabulous four children: Sean, Melanie, Tiffany and Ryan.

To my many writer friends for the great ideas, encouragement, critique, review and counsel. In addition, to all of my friends who listened to me while I plotted out my stories and talked about characters (as though they were real), thank you for letting me bend your ear. Your input has been extremely valuable in making this book better than it was.

ALSO BY LOIS LAVRISA

Liquid Lies

GEORGIA COAST COZY MYSTERIES

Dying for Dinner Rolls

Murderous Muffins

Homicide by Hamlet

Killing with Kings

To purchase, please visit loislavrisa.com/books, or head to your favorite
online bookseller.

CONNECT WITH LOIS

To receive updates on my latest books, including upcoming novels in the Georgia Coast Cozy Mystery series, be sure to sign up for my free author newsletter at **loislavrisa.com/newsletter**.

If you'd like to see what I'm up to on social media, you can find me on Facebook (**facebook.com/authorloislavrisa**), Twitter (**@loislavrisa**), or Instagram (**loislavrisa**).

ABOUT THE AUTHOR

Lois Lavrisa grew up on the rough and tumble South Side of Chicago in a suburb where she spent her childhood summers riding her bike, playing hopscotch, skinning her knees and daydreaming. She earned a Master's and Bachelor of Science in Journalism and Communication with a minor in Public Relations. After college, she wrote training programs for a Fortune 500 company, taught many years as an adjunct professor, and was also a professional cheerleader for the Chicago Bulls. She's been married to her aerospace husband Tom since 1991 and they have four (nearly grown-up) children—two sons and two daughters.

Lois's first novel, *Liquid Lies*, was a finalist for the 2013 Eric Hoffer Award. For her award winning Georgia Coast Cozy Mystery series, set in beautiful historic Savannah, Lois was nominated multiple times for Georgia Author of the Year.

73776440R00105

Made in the USA
Columbia, SC
11 September 2019